DEAD BODY DISPOSAL

JON ATHAN

Copyright © 2021 Jon Athan

All Rights Reserved.

This is a work of fiction. Names, characters, businesses, places, events and incidents are either the products of the author's imagination or used in a fictitious manner. Any resemblance to actual persons, living or dead, or actual events is purely coincidental.

For more information on this book or the author, please visit www.jon-athan.com. General inquiries are welcome.

Facebook: https://www.facebook.com/AuthorJonAthan

Twitter: @Jonny_Athan

Email: info@jon-athan.com

Instagram: @AuthorJonnyAthan

Book cover and logo design by Mibl Art: https://miblart.com/

Thank you for the support!

ISBN: 9798586045966

WARNING

This book contains scenes of intense violence and some disturbing themes. Some parts of this book may be considered violent, cruel, disturbing, or unusual. This book is *not* intended for those easily offended or appalled. Please enjoy at your own discretion.

CONTENTS

Chapter 1	1
Chapter 2	11
Chapter 3	33
Chapter 4	41
Chapter 5	61
Chapter 6	83
Chapter 7	93
Chapter 8	103
Chapter 9	117
Chapter 10	129
Chapter 11	137
Chapter 12	145
Chapter 13	151
Chapter 14	161
Chapter 15	177
Chapter 16	189
Chapter 17	205
Chapter 18	225
JOIN THE MAILING LIST	229
DEAR READER	231

1

WHAT HAVE I DONE?

Panicked breathing. Pacing footsteps. Stifled whimpers.

Max Baker walked back and forth between the foot of the bed and the entertainment center, his trembling hands cupped over his mouth. His knuckles were red and bruised and scraped. Spilling out from his bloodshot eyes with each blink, traces of tears shimmered on his rosy cheeks and trimmed stubble. His curly black hair was soaked in sweat. The sweat left pit stains on his white button-up shirt, too.

He muttered incomprehensibly to himself, words rushing out of his mouth only to be caught in his hands. It sounded like a baby's cooing.

He paced in a hotel room. The entertainment center was connected to a small workstation. Advertisements played on repeat on the muted flat-screen television. The sheets were rolled into a large wrinkled ball on top of the queen-size bed. There was a sitting area with two wingback chairs and a coffee table at the end of the room.

The bathroom and closet, as well as a small table with a vanity mirror, were located close to the room's front door. The workstation—a small space with an ethernet port and plenty of electrical outlets—made the room an 'executive suite.' It was nothing special. If Max had actually visited the hotel during a business trip, he would have complained and asked for an upgrade.

But he wasn't there to discuss taxes with his clients.

He stopped and glanced at the front door, eyes as wide as golf balls. He moved his hands away from his mouth.

He whispered, "Is that him?"

He hurried over to the door, lunging on his tiptoes so as not to alarm any potential visitors of his presence in the room. He peeked through the peephole. There was no one there.

He went back to pacing between the bed and the entertainment center. This time, he massaged his forehead with his fingertips and gripped his waist with his other hand.

Max muttered, "Fuck me... Why did I do that? Why couldn't I just block it out? I didn't want to hurt anyone. I never wanted to hurt anyone... This isn't me. It's not like me." He stopped and stared down at the crimson carpet near the foot of the bed. It was stained with dark spots. He sniffled and whispered, "What have I done?"

Tap, tap, tap!

He turned and looked at the wall behind the television. He heard someone knocking, but it sounded like it was coming from another room. His gaze shifted down to the TV. He could see it was still muted, but he wondered if the knocking sound was somehow coming from the speakers.

Thud! Thud! Thud!

Someone knocked again, harder than the first time. He tiptoed over to the door and looked through the peephole. His frown twisted into a shaky smile.

John Kasper waited in the hallway outside of the room, eyes on his Rolex. He stood six-one, about two inches taller than Max. And as if they had just finished a shift at the same company, they were dressed similarly, too. Kasper wore a light blue shirt with the sleeves rolled up to his elbows, slacks, and dress shoes. His black hair was cut short and neat. He was clean-shaven, flaunting smooth skin, a defined jawline, and strong cheekbones.

Max envied him. He was everything he wished he could be: Rich, strong, tall, confident. But he was convinced that only Kasper could help him out of his predicament. He wiped the tears off his cheeks with the back of his hand, then he opened the door.

With unbridled enthusiasm, Kasper said, "Max, buddy! How are you–" Max grabbed the chest of his shirt and pulled him into the room. Teetering, Kasper said, "Whoa there, pal. Don't pull too hard, this shirt was expensive."

Max slammed the door, turned the lock, and then fastened the swing bar lock. He turned towards Kasper and wagged his index finger at his face. Kasper could see he was disgruntled—so angry and anxious that he couldn't speak. His friend's eyes told tales of sorrow and regret.

He asked, "What happened? What's wrong?"

"What's wrong?" Max repeated in disbelief. He pushed Kasper against the closet door and yelled, "You! You're wrong, Kasper! You're late! You're *always* late when I need you! *Always,* damn it! And then when you do show up—*if* you show up—you bail on me! I don't even know why I called you, man! What the... What the *hell* am I doing?!"

Kasper raised his hands in a peaceful gesture and said, "Take it easy, Max. Seriously, what the fuck's up with you?"

Voice shaking along with his entire body as if he were about to implode, Max said, "Y–You... I–I've... I was... I–I did... I fa... I fucked up. A–And you... you were... You were late, you fa–fucker..."

Kasper squinted an eye and tilted his head to the side. He heard the words, but he didn't understand him. He patted Max's shoulder gently. Max gazed into his friend's shiny blue eyes. He was jealous of those beautiful peepers, too. He covered his face with his hand and started sobbing. Kasper continued patting his back while glancing around the room. He gave him a minute to get it out of his system.

"Max," he said. "Hey, Max. Max, look at me, buddy."

Max kept his head down while wiping his face with his hands. He stepped back until he reached the bathroom doorway, then he looked at Kasper. But he couldn't hold eye contact for longer than a second. He leaned against the doorway and lowered his head in shame.

Kasper said, "I have *no* idea what you're talking about. I mean, I get it, I'm not always on time and sometimes I flake without saying anything, but... Max, man, you called me, like, thirty minutes ago."

Max lifted his head and gazed into Kasper's eyes. He responded, "What? No, that's... It was an hour ago, wasn't it?"

Kasper checked his Rolex, then he shook his head and said, "About thirty minutes ago, buddy."

"Really? I, uh... I could have sworn it was an hour ago."

Kasper smirked and said, "Nope. Honestly, you should be applauding me. I got here faster than most pizza guys this time. Besides, it's not like I agreed to anything. We haven't been planning this for weeks or anything like that, right? *You* called me out of nowhere and told me to be here, and now I'm here. I sound like a great friend if you ask me."

"Yeah, you... you're right."

"Come on, man, what's up with this... mood? You're giving me bad vibes, you know? What's going on? What happened?"

"I messed up."

Kasper gave him a nod and said, "Go on."

Max opened his mouth to speak, but his teeth began to chatter. So, he bit down on his bottom lip so hard that it looked like it was about to burst.

He said, "I lost control of myself. One moment, I was... I was here, I was in *this* room, then the next... I felt like I was watching myself do it. I don't know how it happened, but I did it. And now I'm stuck with no way out."

Kasper grabbed both of Max's shoulders, gave him a little shake, and asked, "*What happened?*"

Max leaned forward and stared at the bed. Kasper looked at it, then back at Max, and then back at the bed. He saw the ball of bedsheets and connected the dots. He huffed, then he chuckled.

He said, "Come on, buddy. You pissed the bed? Didn't want to pay for the housekeeping? Max, pal, I could have just sent you the cash on Venmo or PayPal or something if you needed it. You didn't have to call me down here. Hell, you didn't even have to tell me why, I would have just lent it to you. Can't be that much, can it?"

Max shook his head.

Kasper said, "You... You *didn't* piss the bed? What's up with the bedsheets then?" Max didn't say a word. Kasper shook him again and said, "Hey, stick with me. I can't help you if you can't even tell me what's wrong."

Max said, "Under the bed."

"What about it?"

"Under the bed..."

Kasper knitted his eyebrows at Max—'*What the hell are you talking about?*' He wanted to ask him if he had consumed any alcohol or drugs, but he didn't want to offend him. He walked to the bed while constantly glancing back at his friend. Keeping his shoulder against the doorway, Max stepped out of the bathroom and watched Kasper. His eyes were glassed over, dull and vacant.

Kasper took a knee at the foot of the bed. He spotted the stains on the rug. *Blood or piss?*—he thought. He took one final glance back at Max, then he looked under the bed.

"Oh shit!" he shouted as he fell onto his ass.

Eyes wide and mouth ajar, he crawled backwards. His back hit the entertainment center behind him. He looked at Max, then back at the bed. He saw the pale soles of a woman's feet under it.

He stammered, "Is–Is–Is she–she okay? Is she... Is she o–okay? Wha–Wha... Wha–What did you... Is sh–she..."

He spoke until he was out of breath and light-headed. He grabbed the edge of the table and tried to pull himself up. His clammy hand slipped off the first time. He grabbed it again and struggled to his feet. He staggered towards the coffee table, glancing around as if he were looking for another exit. There was nowhere to run, but at least he couldn't see the body from that angle.

Kasper drew a deep breath, then he pointed at the bed and asked, "Is she okay?"

Max shook his head.

Kasper stuttered, "Is–Is she... Is she dead?"

Max squeezed his eyes shut, frowned, and nodded.

Kasper buried his fingers in his hair and shouted, "Oh shit! What the hell, Max?!"

He stepped towards Max, eager to exit the room, but he didn't want to clash with his friend. He turned and stared at the window over the coffee table. Fear gassed his mind, smothering his rational thoughts and planting seeds of panic in his head. A part of him wanted to jump out through the window. Adrenaline pumped him up.

He considered it for a moment, but he knew he couldn't survive a jump from the 29th floor. He was stronger than Max anyway, so he was safer in the room with him than he was freefalling from the building.

Max put his hands up, as if he were caught red-handed by the police. He walked slowly into the bedroom.

Upon noticing him, Kasper jabbed his finger at him and said, "Stay there. Don't take another step."

"Kasper, please... I need help."

"Yeah, no shit, buddy."

"Your help, Kasper. I need *your* help."

As Max took another step forward, Kasper said, "Don't move, Maxie. Just... Let me think about this, alright? Let me... Let me get my mind right, okay?"

Max clasped his hands in front of his chest and said, "Please help me."

Kasper saw the fear in Max's eyes. It didn't seem like a cold-blooded killing, he had known Max for as long as he could remember and he never seemed like a psychopath, but murder was *murder*. There was no way around that fact. He shook his head and started walking in circles between the bed and the coffee table.

He stopped and said, "I have to go."

"Kasper, *please.*"

"Just get out of the way and let me leave. I won't say a thing about this."

"Don't do this. Please, please, *please* don't leave me like this. I–I called you because I trust you. You're my... my only friend. This was a... an accident. You have to believe me."

Kasper sneered and asked, "What could you possibly need from me? What am I supposed to do to help you? Call the police? Give you a–a–an alibi?"

"Help me get rid of the body."

"Jesus Christ," Kasper responded. He pressed his palms against his face and said, "Ah, shit, you have to be kidding me. You didn't really just say that."

"You're smart. You know how these things work. We used to read about this stuff all the time."

Kasper took his hands off his face and yelled, "*What?!* Are you talking about the books and websites we read in high school? The horror novels? The true crime books? The Wikipedia pages? Are you joking? That was years ago! It was nothing, man! Just reading!"

On the verge of crying again, Max said, "It was research. And I know you remember it. You know everything about this... this morbid crap. You can help me, so *please help me*. Please, Kasper, I'm begging you."

Kasper sighed, then he said, "This is wrong. You... You killed someone. If I help you, I'd... My life, my job... No, I can't be complicit in a murder. Whatever you did, I can't help you."

"My girlfriend... You remember Andrea? Andrea Morales? I dated her in college and we... we're still dating. We live together, we got engaged, and... and she's pregnant. Like five or six months pregnant, Kasper. I can't lose her—*them*—now. This was a... a *big* mistake. I don't know why I did this and I wish I could take it back, but I can't. I need help. Please, man, please."

Kasper was devastated by Max's speech. He had forgotten about Andrea until that very moment. The baby changed everything—babies *always* changed everything. He sat in one of the wingback chairs. He could see the woman's pasty arm under the bed.

He asked, "What happened to you, Max? What did you do?"

Max sat at the foot of the bed across from him. He put his head down and avoided eye contact. He stared at his hands. He had finally stopped shaking. He was ashamed of himself, but he felt a sense of peace around Kasper.

He said, "I called a girl to my room..."

2
WHAT I DID

Panicked breathing. Pacing footsteps. Stifled whimpers.

Max walked back and forth between the foot of the bed and the entertainment center while nibbling on his thumb's fingernail. A coat of sweat glistened on his forehead. He breathed noisily through his nose, although he seemed unaware of all the racket. His heart was doing jumping jacks in his chest, slamming up against his sternum and ribs with each beat.

"Am I really going to do it?" he muttered. "No. No, I'm not. I'm going to pussy out. I always do. Oh God, what am I doing here?"

He stopped and looked at the wall above the bed. He heard something from the darkest corner of his skull.

Tap... tap... tap...

He jogged over to the door, his lips flipping from a smile to a frown and back to a smile again. He looked through the peephole. The sides of his mouth sank into another frown. There was no one there.

As he walked back to the center of the room, he whispered, "Okay, okay, okay. She's not here yet. You're just too excited, Maxie. Calm down. Don't scare her off. Just do what you came here to–"

Thud! Thud! Thud!

The knocking was clear. He returned to the door and took a peek through the peephole. Another smile blossomed on his face. His shoulders loosened and a satisfied sigh escaped his mouth.

Katie Paulson stood in the hallway, chewing on a piece of gum. She was a young woman—mid-twenties, maybe a bit younger. Her short blonde hair barely touched her jawline and the nape of her neck. Her red lipstick harmonized with her bright blue eyes—red and blue like a police siren. There were patches of freckles across her cheekbones, too.

She wore a black leather jacket over an off-white crop top, a short black tube skirt, fishnets, and boots. She wasn't wearing a bra, so her erect nipples were clearly visible through her shirt.

Max opened the door and, struck with a sudden bout of shyness, he stuttered, "He–Hey."

"Hello," Katie responded with a smile. "I'm Katie. And you are...?"

She was vigilant. She didn't make assumptions or answer her own questions. She had heard horror stories of women being tricked into fake taxis and Ubers before ending up dead because they didn't verify the drivers' identities. She needed Max to identify himself before she could trust him.

"I'm Max," Max said. "Um... It's nice to meet you, Katie."

"It's nice to meet you, too, Max. I've really been looking forward to this."

They shook hands, then there was an awkward silence. Max rubbed the back of his neck and grinned, but he looked more like he was gasping for air after winning a marathon.

He said, "You, um... You're taller than I expected."

Katie pouted, then she giggled and nodded. She said, "I'll take that as a compliment. I'm five-eight, thank you very much."

"Oh, that's... that's cool."

"Cool?"

Katie giggled again. She could tell it was his first time meeting a woman like herself. Nervous Johns would normally make her suspicious, but she didn't see any malice in Max's eyes. From her experience, there was no way a man like Max could turn out to be a menace. He was more likely to be a shy virgin than a violent psychopath. She predicted she would discover his unusual fetishes during their time together.

People often hid their sexual desires in fear of going against social norms, so they lived their fantasies out through pornography and prostitution.

Katie asked, "So, may I come inside?"

"Oh! Yeah. Yeah, of course. I'm sorry about that."

"It's no problem at all."

She strutted into the hotel room, simpering. Max watched her for a few seconds, hypnotized by her beauty and comforted by her kindness. He shook his head as he snapped out of his trance. He closed the door behind her, then he opened it again and placed the DO NOT DISTURB sign on the door handle outside, and then he closed and locked it.

Max sat at the foot of the bed, rubbing his clammy palms on his knees. Katie walked around the room, casually checking every nook and cranny. Her safety was her primary concern. To her utter relief, no one else was hiding in the room and there were no obvious attempts at trying to record their meeting.

Max asked, "Did you, um... Did you have any trouble finding the hotel?"

Katie leaned back against the wall in front of him. She said, "No, no. I've actually visited clients here before. It's a nice place, isn't it?"

"You... Did you just say you visited clients here?"

Katie nodded and said, "Yup. The staff isn't so strict about visitors here, so it's good for business. The less busybodies, the better."

"Uh-huh," Max responded, his excitement dying off and his attention wandering to the clock on the nightstand.

He had been hoping for a discrete meeting at a secure location so no one could connect him to her.

Katie mentioned visiting the hotel a couple of times, but she might as well have been a loyal guest with a co-branded credit card and friendly relationship with every staff member.

Noticing his sudden concern, Katie asked, "You okay?"

"Huh? Oh, yeah, I–I'm fine. I'm sorry, I just... Yeah, I'm okay, I just get nervous about things easily. I don't... want to get caught, you know?"

Katie said, "It's okay, hun. I'm going to take care of you. Don't worry about a thing, alright?"

Max looked up at her. She was gentle and sincere. Something about her soft voice calmed him. And her eyes—those beautiful eyes—made him feel human. She wasn't gazing at the monster within him. He had been hoping to meet a greedy, ugly woman with a bad attitude.

It would have made things easier for him.

"Do you mind if I freshen up?" Katie asked. "Don't worry, our time hasn't started yet."

"Yeah, of course. The bathroom is right there. Do you want me to show you?"

With a joyous twinkle in her eye, Katie smirked at him and said, "I think I can find my way, hun. I'll be right back."

As she walked away, Max said, "Oh! And the money is–"

Katie looked back at him and put her index finger up to her lips—*shh*. She winked at him and whispered, "I know."

Max stayed seated, nodding like a bobblehead toy—'*Yeah, yup, of course.*' There were a lot of unspoken rules when it came down to prostitution. One of them was: *Never* mention the money aloud.

Katie entered the bathroom. She moved the shower curtain and found an empty bathtub. An envelope was wedged between the sink's faucet handles and the wall. She opened it up. It was loaded with five one-hundred-dollar bills—her fee for an hour and a half of 'companionship.' She put the envelope in her bag, then she started adjusting her makeup in the mirror.

While scratching his knees in a nervous tic, Max stared at the vanity mirror. He could see the bathroom door from the reflection. *What is she doing in there? Does she need help? Was it enough money? Should I ask?*—he wondered.

He had met Katie through an online message board for men and women searching for companions. That was code for 'prostitutes' in an attempt to skirt the law. Through her profile, he found Katie's social media accounts. She had established a dedicated following by promoting body positivity and sexual freedom. She publicly advocated for the legalization of prostitution and stronger protections for sex workers.

Max respected that about her. She was a public figure, so he assumed she was trustworthy. He was comfortable around people that he trusted and respected. But then it hit him. It was in front of his face the entire time, but it didn't set off any alarms in his head until it was too late. The doubt started to creep into his mind. She had seemed like the perfect candidate for his plot—'*Who's going to miss a hooker?*' But Katie was more than an escort.

She was a person.

A *popular* person.

"She's internet famous," he whispered in awe.

The bathroom door swung open. Katie twirled around the corner. Her bag was slung over her shoulder, but she had stripped down to her panties—a black G-string.

"You ready to have some fun?" she asked.

Max looked shell-shocked, his gaze stuck on the wall in front of him. The same question kept running through his head: *What do I do? What do I do? What do I do?* Katie couldn't read him. She wasn't afraid of him, she still believed he was nothing more than a virgin, but she remained cautious. There was a switchblade and a can of pepper spray in her bag. She set it down on the closest nightstand.

She asked, "Are you okay?" Max didn't respond. Katie put her knee on the bed, stroked his shoulder, and asked, "Are you sure you want to do this? We can always just talk, you know?"

Max looked at her and asked, "How did you know what I was thinking?"

Katie smiled nervously, furrowed her brow, and asked, "What do you mean?"

"You asked... You asked if I was sure I wanted to go through with this. I was *just* thinking that. I don't know if I can do it."

"Oh. I just guessed this was your first time with a woman like me."

"Huh?"

"You know, everyone's nervous during their first time. It's nothing to be ashamed of. Come on, we can take it slow."

Tears glazing his eyes, he stuttered, "I–I meant the other thi–"

Mid-sentence, Katie mounted his lap. She wrapped her arms around his neck and kissed him passionately. Max wanted to say: '*I meant the other thing.*' And by 'the other thing,' he meant *murder*. He was starting to question whether he could commit a murder or not. There was more to think about, more to plan. He went there based off an intrusive thought.

I don't have to do it, he told himself. *I can just walk away. Or I can just fuck her and get it over with. But I don't have to kill her. No one has to die. I was wrong. I'm okay now.*

Katie gently pushed him back against the bed. She unbuckled his belt and unbuttoned his fly, then she pulled his pants down to his ankles. She glided her palms across his thighs and leaned close to his crotch. She caressed his penis with her warm breath. Yet, through his gray boxer briefs, she could see he was flaccid.

She hooked her fingers under his waistband, then she slid his underwear down. As expected, his penis was still soft, the glans hiding under his foreskin. His dick looked like an anteater's snout sticking out of a trimmed lawn. She didn't find it funny. She was a caring, understanding person. But she had to choose her words and actions wisely.

The ego was a sensitive beast. One wrong word—one uncertain facial expression—could aggravate a person's insecurities and incite a violent response.

She kissed his pubic region. She avoided touching his dick with her hands. If she had tried to arouse him with a handjob, it would have only required her thumb and index finger. At that point, it would have looked like she was playing the world's smallest violin. She didn't want to plant that image in his head. She licked his scrotum up and down, then she slurped his dick into her mouth.

She managed to roll his foreskin back with her tongue. He grew semi-erect in her mouth, but he wasn't hard enough to wear a condom or even penetrate her.

Max blamed the guilt tearing away at his heart. He had a pregnant fiancé at home. Adultery wasn't part of the plan.

Do it, he thought.

He heard it in his head as his voice, but it didn't feel like *his* thought. He felt like the idea was injected into his brain by someone else. And it was tangible. It was crawling in his skull, scrambling through the sulci of his brain and repeating the same demand over and over.

Do it. Do it. Do it.

He closed his eyes and shook his head, tears rolling

down the sides of his face and wetting his hair. Now his *own* thoughts were colliding with the *intruding* thoughts. Voices clashed in his head, creating a deafening argument.

Do it. Don't do it. Do it. Don't do it. Do it! Don't do it! Do it! Do it! Do it!

He let out a long groan. Katie mistook it as a moan of pleasure. His penis had become erect in her mouth after all. But Max had lost control of himself. The guilt checked out of his heart—and the depravity checked in.

Eyes closed, focused on pleasuring her client, Katie didn't see it coming. She sucked Max's dick, bobbing her head while stroking the shaft. Max sat up and struck her with a powerful hook. His fist hit the left side of her head, leaving her ear buzzing while also causing her to inadvertently bite down on his penis.

Max screamed through his gritted teeth while pulling his dick out of her mouth. Her teeth scraped the shaft of his penis—three thin cuts on top, two on the bottom. One of her canine's nicked the crown of his glans.

Katie fell back, her head ringing. She held her hand over her buzzing ear and whined. She tasted the blood in her mouth. She thought it was coming from her gums, but all blood shared the same flavor profile —metallic and salty. It didn't matter if it came from someone's thumb or genitals. In this case, she was tasting the blood from Max's penis.

She felt like time had paused for a moment as she faced a fight-or-flight situation. Max was a foot away from her, bawling as he glared at his sliced penis. She could have sprinted to the door and yelled for help, but her bag was closer. The pepper spray seemed like her best option. If she couldn't spray it at his face, she could at least shower his dick with it.

Gonorrhea couldn't compete with pepper spray in a urethra.

She scrambled to the nightstand and cried, "Help! Hel–"

With his pants around his ankles, Max grabbed a fistful of her hair and yanked her back before she could reach her bag. He slammed her against the wall, then he gripped her throat in his left hand to pin her against it. Katie kneed him. She was aiming for his crotch, but she hit his thigh instead. Max slapped her with all of his might. The *whack* was so loud that it could be heard from the hallway.

But there were no other guests out there.

Katie's left cheek was redder than the other. She tried to scream, but she couldn't breathe with Max's fingers buried in her throat. She writhed against the wall, feet and elbows *thudding* on it. She kneed him again. Her knee landed against his pubic region, causing him to stagger back a bit and recoil out of fear.

Max slapped her a second time. Then he hit her a *third* time and a *fourth* time and a *fifth* time. Her cheek went from candy apple red to burgundy, and her freckles were replaced with petechiae.

Katie planted her right foot on the wall, then she kicked herself off it and launched her knee at Max's crotch—*bullseye*.

"Ow!" Max cried as he stumbled back.

He put his knees together and covered his genitals with his hands while whimpering. Katie fell to her hands and knees, drawing one raspy breath after another. She was dizzy and lethargic from the lack of oxygen. She pushed herself up to her feet only to collapse after taking one step forward. So, she crawled towards the door.

Max pulled his pants up and went after her. He grabbed another handful of her hair and dragged her back, pulling her up to her feet in the process. Katie extended her arm forward and reached for the door, as if she believed her arm could magically stretch over three meters to touch the handle. She saw the door moving farther and farther away from her. She clawed at Max's forearm with her other hand.

She panted, "He–He–He..." Max hissed and loosened his grip as her fingernails cut his skin. She screamed, "Help!"

He pushed her down, then he spun her around and thrust her head at the bed's footrest. The entire bed shook upon impact. The edge of the footrest cut her left temple open, painting her blonde locks red. Some of the blood trickled onto the rug. He slammed her head against the footrest repeatedly, using her skull like a battering ram.

The wall behind the bed *thudded*, but it didn't come from his room. The neighbor, fed up by the noise, banged on the wall.

Max released Katie's hair. Her body hit the floor. She drifted in and out of consciousness. Max looked at his hand. Some strands of the escort's bloody hair were wrapped around his fingers.

"Oh my God," he said shakily. "Oh God, no. What the hell did I do?"

He buckled his belt as he rushed into the bathroom. He washed his hands with warm water at the sink, then he washed his hands again with steaming hot water and soap. The hair and blood came off his hands. As he turned to leave, a thought hit him: *No, the hair is still in the drain. Someone will find it if it's not completely washed away!* He ran back to the sink and turned the faucet on again.

Face scrunched up with concern, he watched as the water splashed and swirled down the drain. He couldn't see past the drain stopper, though.

Meanwhile, in the bedroom, Katie got up to her hands and knees. The head trauma left her nauseous and lightheaded. She knew she couldn't run out of the room because she couldn't outrun or overpower Max. Her best options were the self-defense weapons in her bag and the telephone—*'Get armed and get help.'*

She pulled herself over the footrest and onto the bed, blood dribbling down the left side of her face. Her eyes were open to slits as she fought off her drowsiness. She crawled forward, but she was too weak to stay on her hands and knees. Refusing to quit, she wiggled towards the nightstand. Her vision was distorted, blurring and focusing in a pulsing rhythm.

She saw the numbers on the clock: *8:14 PM*.

Max's eyes bulged upon hearing the bed squeak. He lurched out of the bathroom, leaving the faucet running. He pounced on Katie just as she reached for the nightstand.

"Stop!" he yelled as he straddled her waist. "Stop it! Don't make me do this!"

Squirming under him, voice weakened by Max's weight on top of her, Katie whined, "S–Somebody help me... Ga–God, help me..."

She managed to roll onto her side. Some blood had entered her left eye, making it look like she was shedding crimson tears. She stretched her arm out as far as possible. Her fingertips touched the phone's coiled cord.

"Stop it!" Max barked. "Stop, you cunt!"

He punched her face. Blood squirted out of the gash on her temple. Katie unleashed a long, pained groan as she rolled under him. She ended up on her back, his knees around her ribs. He hesitated to hit her again. Blood lined her teeth and tinted her enamel pink. The cut on her temple was deep. He saw a slit of white in it.

He thought: *Her skull? No way. I couldn't have done that.*

"Don't kill me," she squeaked out.

Frowning, Max said, "I don't have a choice."

"Please... I don't want to die. I don't want–"

Max grunted as he punched her again. He attacked her with a barrage of jabs, cycling between lefts and rights. He drummed his fists against her face, playing a song of dull *thuds* and *tacks*. He put his shoulder into each blow, trying to hit her as hard as possible, as if he had a lifelong vendetta against her—as if he *really* hated her.

But he hardly knew the poor woman. And she was kind to him throughout their entire professional relationship.

The petechiae on Katie's cheek worsened. It was now a wide patch of blood under her skin. The freckles were gone. A wide, deep gash stretched over her left eyebrow. Blood spilled into her eye sockets, turning her vision red and blurry. Her nose broke, curved like a capital 'C.' The bridge of her nose was cut and blood flowed out of her crushed nostrils.

Max started to sweat again. Beating a person to the brink of death was exhausting. There was a feral yet determined look in his eyes. He was a vicious animal—but a vicious animal with a *premeditated* purpose. He couldn't stop.

Between punches, he grunted, "I... don't... have... a... *choice!*"

He chipped some of her incisor teeth. She swallowed the broken pieces along with mouthfuls of blood. She was left with a mouth of jagged sawtooth teeth. Her teeth and his fists cut her swollen lips. He punched her so hard at an angle that he tore a chunk of flesh off her right cheekbone. He could see another slit of white in the deep cut.

He stopped beating her for a moment, growling with each heavy breath. His hands trembled as stabs of pain throbbed in his broken, lacerated knuckles. The pain surged through his hands and entered his forearms before dying out at his elbows. It made his arms ache. His knuckles and fingers were covered in blood—*his and hers*.

A tear plopped on one of his hands as he stared down at them. Then he clenched his fists, ground his teeth, and screamed, veins bulging from his brow and neck. He punched her one more time—her nose crunching from the jab—then he fell beside her. He buried his face in the bedsheets and sobbed. He apologized to her, but his words were incomprehensible.

Katie was unconscious. Her lips fluttered and blood spurted out of her mouth with each wheeze. Her face had ballooned during the beating, bumpy like a rugged potato. Her eyes were swollen shut, but her eyelids continued twitching, revealing her blood-red sclerae. Blood from her facial wounds had rolled into her scalp, streaking her hair.

Max got on his hands and knees. A string of drool hung from his gaping mouth. He was rendered speechless by his violent acts. But the voice in his head continued speaking.

Do it!

He grabbed the digital clock from the nightstand and tugged on it until it disconnected from the wall. It was flimsy, but it was the first object that popped into his mind. He held it over his head, then he swung it down at Katie's face repeatedly. It *clinked* and *clanked* with each hit. The sharp edge of the clock sliced her face and widened her other wounds.

The cut on the bridge of her nose deepened until her nasal septum was severed. The tip of her nose was mashed down, almost touching her upper lip. Another horizontal cut stretched across her glabella, connecting her blonde eyebrows.

The clock's cheap frame cracked. A screw flew onto the bed, then one of the button's snapped off, then the LCD screen shattered. Upon hitting her forehead for the thirteenth time, the clock burst. Some wires stuck out of it.

Max stopped hitting her again. He watched her face carefully. Her eyelids stopped twitching and her lips stopped fluttering. He frowned, then he smiled. *It's over,* he told himself. Then he felt her chest move. He dismounted her and gazed at her bare breasts. His frown returned as her chest rose ever so slightly.

She was beaten until she was unrecognizable, it looked like her head had been dipped into a large-capacity blender and 'blended' for several minutes, but she still clung to life. She was a fighter.

Max sat beside her and covered his mouth with both of his hands. Rocking back and forth, his voice muffled, he whimpered, "What did I do? What did I do? Oh, fuck me... fuck me... Why did I come here?" He glanced at the escort's disfigured face, then he quickly looked away. Voice cracking, he said, "I'm so sorry. I'll... I have to... I–I'll call an ambulance. I'll make this right. I'll f–f–fix this."

Just as he reached for the phone on the nightstand, another thought invaded his mind: *Finish it.*

"I can't," he whispered, hand hovering over the phone.

Finish it, the thought repeated itself in his mind.

His hand trembled over the phone, causing him to tap it, but he couldn't grab it. He lost the battle within himself again. Crying, he crawled onto the bed. He sat near the headboard and placed Katie's head on his lap. Then he wrapped the clock's thick cord around her neck. Katie let out a short gasp as he tugged on the cord. It was as if her last breath had been squeezed out of her throat.

Max had seen the documentaries and news reports. He had read the true crime books and articles. He knew strangulation took time.

Her chest immediately stopped moving. She couldn't draw another breath. For about a minute, her fingers and toes curled a bit. After two minutes, her eyes became motionless under her eyelids. After three minutes, the croaking and gurgling sounds coming out of her mouth stopped. Her neck started turning red and purple. Her skin appeared ashen between the rivers of blood flowing across her face. Her lips, big and cut, were discolored, too.

Five minutes passed.

Max was certain brain death had already occurred, but he kept strangling her for another minute just to be safe. He released the cord and sighed. He leaned back against the headboard and stared vacantly at Katie's mushy face. He cocked his head to the side. His eyelids began to flicker. Reality morphed before his very eyes. One second, he saw Katie's beautiful, unscathed face smiling up at him. The next, he saw the truth: A dead prostitute on his lap.

He staggered off the bed. He noticed the steam coming out of the bathroom. The water from the running faucet was boiling hot—exactly what he needed. He washed his hands in the scalding water until his skin was bright red and numb. Her blood was gone, but the cuts on his knuckles kept bleeding. He pressed some wet wads of toilet paper against the wounds—makeshift Band-Aids.

"I–I–I have to go," he stammered.

He reached for the door handle, but he stopped upon hearing a set of lumbering footsteps outside. He looked through the peephole. There was no one there. He hurried to the other end of the room. He gazed at the window and considered climbing out, but he knew it was sealed shut. Breaking the window would have alarmed the hotel's employees. And he didn't have the skill or the strength to climb down 29 floors anyway.

He marched over to the nightstand. He caught a glimpse of Katie's face from the corner of his eye. He looked away and whined quietly. He looked through the contacts on his phone.

'*Andrea Morales*'—He thought about calling his fiancé. He wanted to hear her gentle voice say: '*Everything's going to be okay. I forgive you.*' But he couldn't arouse any suspicion. He certainly couldn't ask her for help.

'*Hey, honey... Oh, the business meeting? It went well. Hey, listen, um... I killed someone in my hotel room... Yeah, just an escort... Any ideas on how to get rid of the body?*'

It was an absurd idea. His thumb went over to the contact labeled '*Mom.*' He had a healthy relationship with his parents, but they couldn't help him. They weren't trained to dispose of dead bodies after all. He didn't want to endanger his family, either. He stopped on the contact labeled '*John Kasper.*'

Kasper was his friend. He was close enough to be trusted, but not close enough to be considered family, so Max didn't feel *too* guilty about dragging him into his situation. He remembered all of the morbid conversations they had shared in the past, too. If anyone could help him out, it was Kasper.

He called his number and listened to the ringback tone as he paced beside the bed. The ringing drilled into one ear and came out of the other, obnoxious and deafening. He was sent to voicemail.

He smiled, as if Kasper could see him, and he stuttered, "Ka–Kasper, um... Hey, it's, uh... It's Max. Max Baker. I, um... I need to see you, man. I need to see you as soon as possible. Like, in, um... Let's say thirty minutes. Meet me at the Club Edison Hotel. Room 2906. You don't need to talk to the front desk clerk. Actually, just... just don't talk to *anyone*, okay? Go straight to the room and I'll be here. Please come and... and please hurry. Thank you."

He disconnected from the call. He stood there with a thousand-yard stare, gazing at the light pinstripe wall in front of him. His face knotted and tears dripped from the corners of his eyes. The murder took a toll on his psyche. He had planned it all out, but a *thought* was different from an *action*. Everyone was a killer until it was time to kill. He barreled into the bathroom and vomited in the toilet.

3

WHAT DO WE DO NOW?

"After that, I took her underwear off and I grabbed her clothes from the bathroom," Max said, staring at some dark spots on the rug. "It was already folded. She was a clean... and nice person. I put her on the floor and rolled her under the bed. Then I wrapped the bedsheets around her belongings. I tossed the clock in there, too. The bedsheets were bloody anyway, so I was going to burn it all. Maybe in this bathtub or some ditch in the woods if I could sneak it all out. I don't know, I didn't really think that far. And then... Then you showed up. That's what happened. That's what I did, Kasper."

Kasper couldn't hide his astonishment. His mouth hung ajar, his eyes were wide open, and his eyebrows were raised. He glanced at the vacant seat to his right, as if he were communicating with an invisible man: *'You believe this guy?'* He looked back at Max and shook his head, a mixture of disbelief and disappointment brewing inside of him. Close to tears, Max pulled his frowning lips into his mouth and nodded, as if to say: '*I know, I know, I'm a monster.*' He was ashamed and afraid of himself. They sat in silence for about a minute.

Max said, "I'm sorry about all of this. I know you think I'm a bad person. Shit, man, *I know* I'm a bad person. You don't have any real reason to help me... but I need help. I'll find a way to make this right—I'll pay her family, I'll donate to charity, I'll turn myself in someday—but I can't do that now. Andrea, my unborn baby, *my family*... They need me. I need to get out of this. I need to buy some time. And–And... And if things go wrong, I'll take full responsibility. I'll say I forced you to help me. 'I threatened him,' that's what I'll tell them. Can you help me out? For old times' sake?"

'*For old times' sake.*' The term was used to acknowledge pleasant memories or a shared past. But Max and Kasper never killed anyone or disposed of a dead body together before.

There was another minute of silence.

Kasper said, "You used to talk about some messed up shit, Max. And that's what I thought it was: Shit. *Bullshit*. I remember what you said in high school and college and at that party a few years ago. You said, 'I want to kill someone someday.' Remember?" Max tried to say something, but only a dry croak came out. Kasper said, "Okay, maybe you didn't say those exact words, but that was what you *said*. It was what you meant, and you can't deny that. I thought it was just... I thought we were shooting the shit. Just fucking around, you know? I never thought you'd go through with it."

"I never thought I'd go through with it, either. I just couldn't control myself. I mean, you're right. I always had that thought at the back of my mind, but it wasn't supposed to happen. It was just a thought and it just... consumed me recently. I couldn't get it out of my head. If it wasn't her, it would have been..."

He couldn't finish the sentence. He knew what he wanted to say, but he didn't want to hear himself say it. He sniffled and wiped his face.

Max said, "It was like I was possessed."

"I just... can't believe you did this."

"I can't believe it myself. But you have to believe me: It was a *big* mistake."

"How could it be a mistake? You said you beat her to a pulp with your fists and then strangled her, Max. You said you strangled her for more than *five* minutes. You had plenty of time to stop and call the police. For Christ's sake, you killed someone. I don't know how to... to process this, man. It's like... I never expected it, but I *kinda* expected it. Just not today and not like this. I didn't think you'd call me, either. I'm just... I'm... I'm nobody, bro."

Kasper chuckled, then he kept rambling about himself. Max stopped listening to him. He knew Kasper was scared, confused, and nervous, much like himself.

"Kasper," Max interrupted. Kasper stopped smiling, face tightening with concern. Max said, "Tell me what to do. How do I get out of this?"

Kasper shrugged, then he said, "Buddy, I guess you... you come clean or you run. Right?"

"I can't do that!" Max yelled while jumping to his feet. He thrust his finger at Kasper and shouted, "Haven't you been listening?! I can't go to prison! Not now! What about Andrea? What about our baby? My job? I–I can't just throw my life away, man! I fucked up tonight, but I can't let this fuck up the rest of my life!"

Kasper shrank into his seat, raised his hands above his shoulders, and said, "Calm down, buddy."

"Don't tell me to calm down! I called you to help me and you're telling me to turn myself in! You're telling me to fuck myself and go straight to prison! You can't ask me to–"

"Max, *calm down*," Kasper said sternly. "You're fucking yourself by screaming. What do you think your neighbors are doing right now? They're annoyed and they're probably calling the front desk. Stop freaking out. For fuck's sake, you're the last person here that should be throwing a tantrum in the first place. *You* did this to yourself and *you* dragged me into this. So, stop yelling before you get us both in trouble. Okay? *Okay?*"

Max shut his mouth and breathed through his nose. He was angry at Kasper, but his point was proven. Kasper was a smart, level-headed person. He was in trouble, his presence at the crime scene was enough to implicate him, but he was calm. Panicking caused more problems than it ever solved.

Pacing between the bed and the coffee table, Max said, "You see, you're good at this sort of stuff. When we were younger, you knew how to get out of trouble. You'd convince me to steal a pack of cigarettes or some beer because that's just what you'd do. I'd get caught, but you'd disappear." He stopped in front of his friend. He knelt in front of him, as if he were about to propose to him, and he said, "What if you were in my shoes? And what if prison or running weren't options? How would *you* get out of this?"

Kasper puckered his lips and scratched his chin. He glanced at the body under the bed, then he looked away. He examined the room. The front door was the only exit.

He sighed, then he said, "Listen, Max, people get caught in situations like this because of *DNA*. Fingerprints, hair, bodily fluids... Hell, man, they can probably track you from the air that comes out of your lungs these days. You're going to have to clean this place up. And I mean *really* clean it up. But right now, the elephant in the room is your biggest problem. If you can't get rid of the 'elephant' quietly, then there's no point in doing anything else. So, as much as it pains me to say it... you have to get rid of the body."

"Yeah, that's what I was thinking, but I don't know how to do that."

"Well, um... Let's think. You can't drag her out through the lobby, can you? Even if you could, where would you take her? Sometimes, the best hiding place is in plain sight."

"So... I should hide her in this room?"

"No, but you're on the right track," Kasper said. He leaned forward with his elbows on his knees. He said, "I remember hearing about a girl—a Canadian student. She went to California on vacation or something like that. She was caught by a security camera acting erratically in an elevator at some hotel. Then she vanished. *Poof!* You know what happened to her? Where she was found?"

Max squinted, nodded, and said, "I think I remember seeing that video. She died, right?"

"She was found dead in a water tank at the top of her hotel. She vanished there and she was found there, but it took them weeks to get to the bottom of it. So, if I were you, I'd put her on the roof. If there's a water tank up there, I'd put her in there. And if that doesn't work... I guess I'd put her in my luggage, roll her out through the lobby, then find somewhere else to dump her. It would buy time. That's the most important thing right now. You can decide to fess up or run or *whatever* later."

"That can work. Yeah, I can do that."

A newfound sense of determination sparked in his eyes. He crawled over to the bed and pulled on Katie's leg and arm, dragging her out inch by inch. She had been laying on her stomach because Max didn't want to see her injuries.

"She's heavier than I thought," Max said. He beckoned to Kasper and asked, "Can you give me a hand?"

"No," Kasper said bluntly.

"What? Why?"

"I have to look out for myself here, buddy. I'm taking a big risk already by sticking around and 'advising' you. I can keep doing that, but I won't touch her or you. I can't afford to put my DNA on her. You said it yourself: I'm good at staying out of trouble. If anything goes wrong, I'm not going down with you, Max."

"I guess you're right about that, too. I'm sorry for bringing you here."

Kasper smirked and said, "Someone has to keep us out of prison, eh?"

Max returned the smile and said, "Thank you."

"Don't mention it until we're in the clear. Get moving, buddy."

Max rubbed his nose with the back of his hand. He grimaced as his knuckles ached and stung. He pulled on the corpse again.

4

DEAD BODY TRANSPORTATION

Max groaned as he pulled on Katie's arm and leg. He leaned back, leveraging his weight to help him. Her body moved an inch and then another, then Max fell on his ass between the wingback chairs as Katie's nude body slid out. Her bloody face left a dark streak on the rug. A powerful stench came out from under the bed with her. Urine glistened on her thighs and feces stained her ass cheeks.

Max whispered, "Oh my…"

Kasper looked away and said, "It happens. Her muscles are relaxing, so her body emptied her bladder and bowels. Rigor mortis is next. You should move her now before she stiffens up."

"I did this to her…"

"*Max,* move her before the rigor mortis sets in."

"Yeah, yeah, I–I understand," Max said as a single tear rolled down his cheek. He stood up and said, "Let me just clean her up first."

"Are you listening to me? The rigor mortis, Max. It's going to make it *very* difficult for you. You should–"

"I can't just dump her like this," Max interrupted. As he walked to the bathroom, he said, "I killed her. I took her away from her family and friends. If I'm going to dump her, I should dump her with some dignity. Some respect, you know?"

Kasper sank into his seat, shook his head, and sighed. Max rolled up a thick wad of toilet paper. He ran some warm water over it, then he went back to the bedroom. He cleaned the feces off her ass first, then he rolled up the wad and used the other side to wipe the urine away. While doing so, he noticed the piss stain on the rug under the bed.

"I'm going to need some vinegar and a brush to get these stains out," he said.

"You might need one of those heavy-duty carpet cleaners if I'm being honest."

"Let's hope not. People would definitely notice that."

Kasper said, "I guess you could piss over it and call housekeeping. Tell 'em you pissed under the bed and they'll clean it up for you."

Max huffed, then he asked, "And how would I explain that? An 'accident' on the bed? Sure, it happens. An 'accident' *under* the bed? Doesn't sound normal to me."

"Doesn't matter. I don't think they'd ask too many questions unless you refuse to pay for the damages. Money can make all of your problems go away."

Max went back to the bathroom and flushed the wad of dirty paper down the toilet, then he returned to the bedroom. He wondered why Kasper was suddenly so calm and quiet. There was a dead body at his feet, but he didn't seem so disturbed anymore.

"So, should I, um... How should I get her up there?" Max asked. "Should I wrap her in the bedsheets and just carry her out?'

Kasper responded, "The body's going to be found sooner or later. If the bedsheets or *anything* from this room are found with her, they'll track it all back to Room 2906 and they'll start linking everything to you. You don't want to make it easy for the police, right?"

"Then what should I do?"

"For now, you should make it look natural. Prop her up against you with her face on your chest. Make it look like she's some drunk chick you picked up at a bar and you're just trying to get her to the lobby after a one-night stand. Take her to the stairwell. It's just down the hall, next to the vending machines. You only have to go up past the thirtieth floor, then you're on the roof. From there, all you have to do is find somewhere to hide her—like a water tank. Got it?"

"Okay, so should I dress her or cover her up with something?"

"No point and no time. She's dead and she *looks* dead. Some clothes aren't going to change that. If anyone gets a good look at her, it's over. So, just cover her up with your body and move quickly."

Max stuttered, "Bu–But what about the cameras? What am I going–"

"Max, you don't have time to think of an excuse for every potential outcome. Anything can happen. Andrea could show up if she was even *a little* suspicious about you. A neighbor could have called the front desk or the *police* if you bothered him enough with your screaming. Get rid of the elephant in the room, then deal with the little details."

Nodding rapidly, Max said, "Yeah, yeah, yeah. You're totally right. I have to do this."

He rolled Katie onto her back and recoiled upon catching a glimpse of her swollen, bloody face. He closed his eyes and took a deep breath, then he hooked his arms under her armpits and lifted her from the floor. Dead bodies felt heavier because of their downward force. Without any assistance from her, he teetered to keep his balance. He leaned back against the wall beside the entertainment center, then he wrapped his arms around her torso and held her in a tight bear hug.

He staggered backwards towards the front door, Katie's limp feet gliding across the floor. He looked through the peephole. The hallway was empty. He didn't hear anyone out there, either.

He glanced over at Kasper in search of some reassurance. Kasper stayed seated. He only nodded at him —*'Go on, do it.'*

Max breathed in sharply, then he opened the door and stumbled out of the room with Katie in his arms.

He crashed into a wall across the hall, narrowly avoiding the door to Room 2907. Katie slid down against his torso, her blood staining his shirt. He adjusted his arms, lifted her up, then tightened his grip around her. He looked over his shoulder, then straight ahead.

He could see he was only three rooms away—about twenty-five meters—from the vending machines. He pushed himself off the wall and lumbered forward. His footsteps were heavy but not unusual. Yet, to him, each footstep sounded like a volcanic eruption. He felt like the receptionists could hear him walking from the lobby.

Five steps later, he staggered again. He leaned against the wall between Room 2907 and 2905. He breathed heavily, like a pregnant woman in labor. Katie's hair, matted with dried blood, moved with each wheeze. Sweat dripped across his brow and tickled the nape of his neck. His heart raced, pounding his sternum like a boxer punching a speed bag.

He took two more steps forward while leaning against the wall, then he stopped and furrowed his brow.

"Wha–What the hell?" he stuttered, barely audible.

The hallway appeared to be extending with every step. He squeezed his eyes shut tightly, as if that would fix his vision. He jerked his head back as he opened his eyes. The vending machines looked like they were thirty meters away now. He muttered incomprehensibly as he shambled forward. He squinted at the floor.

The diamond-pattern rug appeared to be stretching, too. He stumbled to the center of the corridor. Wide-eyed, he glared back at the wall. He felt like someone—*or something*—had pushed him off it. He glanced over at the parallel wall, then at the floor. The hallway—the *entire* hallway—looked like it was tilting to the right.

He moved forward as quickly as possible. He found himself teetering towards the right side of the corridor. He approached the door to Room 2904. Then the hallway started tilting to the left, so *he* stumbled to the left side of the hall. Room 2903 was just a few feet away. Yet, it looked like the vending machines were now sixty meters away.

Eyes bulging from their sockets, Max said, "What the hell is—"

He gasped as the door to Room 2901 cracked open an inch. He dropped Katie. She fell to her knees in front of him, her face against his crotch. It looked like she was performing fellatio on him, her bare legs sprawled across the carpet. He picked her up and turned around, trying to use his body to hide hers.

"No, no, no, no, no," he muttered.

He heard the door's hinges behind him. *Don't look, don't look, don't look,* he told himself. *He won't notice you if you pretend like you didn't notice him.* But his curiosity got the best of him. He slowly turned his head until he could peek over his shoulder.

A young black man, dressed in a tracksuit, exited Room 2901. He plugged his Bluetooth earbuds into his ears and looked over at Max. It was a split-second glance, like someone checking for traffic before crossing a street, but Max saw it as a long, steely glare.

"My–My girlfriend... Sh–She–She's my girlfriend," Max stammered.

The man didn't notice them. He pulled his cell phone out of his pocket and started playing music through his earbuds, then he checked his text messages.

Max said, "She's, um... She's just a little drunk. Those cocktails... They're too strong for her, but she loves 'em. She's okay, though. She's alright. I–I'm taking her back to her room." The other guest didn't hear a word. He turned the corner at the end of the hall and headed to the elevators. A little louder but not quite screaming, Max said, "Yeah! She'll be okay!"

There was no answer because there was no one there. The other guest was long gone by then, leaving Max in a disquieting dead silence. The young man was heading out for a jog before planning to meet some friends for a drink. He didn't notice the killer carrying a dead body in the hallway outside of his hotel room.

Thanks to cell phones, people stopped noticing the 'little' things in life.

Max stared at the vending machines. He was just one room away from reaching the emergency stairwell, but he got cold feet. Doubt infected his mind and fear weakened his heart. If he couldn't handle another guest, there was no way he could deal with any of the hotel employees if he ran into them. He needed a new strategy.

He hurried back down the hall. He tapped his keycard on the door lock, pushed the door open, then stumbled into his room with Katie's corpse in his arms.

"What happened?" Kasper asked as he stood from his seat.

"Shit!" Max yelled as he lost his footing. Katie's body fell out of his arms and hit the floor between the foot of the bed and the entertainment center. Max barked, "Goddammit! God *fucking* damn it! He almost–"

He stopped upon noticing Katie's gnarled face. Due to the bumps and blood, he couldn't even see her eyes. There were thin crevices between the mounds of swollen flesh across her entire face. He rolled her over, then he paced between the bathroom door and the closet. He ran his fingers through his hair, then he gripped the nape of his neck with both hands.

"It's over, it's all over," he muttered. "I screwed up, man."

"What happened?" Kasper repeated.

"I screwed up!"

Kasper raised a hand at him and said, "Calm down. You're going to–"

"He saw me! Someone saw me!"

"Max, stop yelling."

"He's going to tell the front desk! They're going to tell the cops! And then the cops are going to come here! I fucked it all up!"

Kasper lunged over Katie's corpse, then he rushed towards Max. He grabbed Max's shoulders and shook him gently.

He said, "Hey—*hey*—you need to calm down."

"I can't," Max whined, his legs moving unsteadily under him. "It–It's over, man. They're going to arrest me and... and... and my life is over. I fucked up."

Shh, shh—Kasper shushed him, like a mother soothing a newborn baby. He patted Max's shoulder and said, "You're overreacting."

"I'm not... It's really over."

"No one saw you, buddy. Maybe they looked your way, but they didn't *see* you. It's like, um... You might *hear* someone speaking to you, but you might not be *listening*. You get me? No, he didn't see you, Max. If he saw you, there would have been a big commotion. He would have ran or hurried away. We would be hearing sirens right now. So, tell me: Did he run? Did he look scared?"

Max blinked one eye at a time as he tried to recollect the encounter in the hallway. It felt like it had happened years ago—*a distant memory*. He sniffled and shook his head.

"Good," Kasper said. "Do you hear any sirens?"

"N–No, I guess not."

"You guess not? Do you hear any sirens or not?"

"*No.* No, I don't."

"Exactly. You're okay. He didn't see you or her. You'll only screw yourself if you keep screaming, so quit it. You understand?"

Max nodded reluctantly. He grabbed some tissue from the table in front of the vanity mirror to wipe his eyes and blow his nose. Kasper stepped over Katie's body and returned to the chair next to the coffee table. He tapped his index finger against his lips as he scanned the room. He sought another transportation method, but he didn't see anything useful.

He sighed, then he said, "If you really want to get rid of the body, you're going to have to try again."

"I can't just carry her out like that. It's way too obvious. And she's too heavy for me. I can't move fast enough to avoid the other guests."

"Okay, well, let's think of another way to move her. Any ideas?"

"I think we should wrap her in the bedsheets. We carry her out to the roof, we unwrap her... we dump her in a water tank or somewhere safe... and then we bring the bedsheets back to the room."

Kasper responded, "I guess that can work. *But* I have two issues with your plan."

"What is it?"

"First of all, it's risky. You said someone looked your way in the hall. You see, he didn't notice you because there's nothing unusual about... *people*. He sees people every day—like you, like me, like your escort. Even if he noticed she was naked, he could have thought of you as a 'kinky' couple and maybe that even scared him off. He didn't want anything to do with *people like you*. You get what I'm saying? Now, if you go out there with a dead body wrapped in bloody bedsheets, it's going to look like you're dragging a *dead body wrapped in bloody bedsheets*. You might as well be dragging a damn body-bag through the building, Max. It's *too* conspicuous."

While breathing through his nose, Max bit his thumb's fingernail and nodded. Kasper's rationale made sense to him.

Kasper said, "Secondly, you kept saying 'we.' '*We* carry her, *we* unwrap her, *we* dump her...' I told you already: I can't touch her. It's out of the question. We have to think of another way."

Max walked around the room and searched for another escape route. There was a ventilation shaft in the upper corner of the room, but it was too small to fit a corpse. He stopped in the bathroom doorway and stared at the bathtub. He had seen several movies and TV shows depicting the disposal of dead bodies in tubs full of acid.

Kasper said, "Max."

Max flinched and looked over his shoulder. Kasper's voice sounded like it came from behind him, but there was no one there. Eyes squinched down into slits, confused but curious, he returned to the bedroom and found Kasper sitting in the same seat.

Kasper said, "Let me ask you something. You came here on business, right?"

"No, not exactly. I came to... to meet *her*."

"I know that, but you told Andrea you were going out on business, correct?"

"Yeah, so?"

"So, where's your luggage?'

"My lug..."

Mid-sentence, the pieces to the puzzle connected in his head. *My luggage,* he thought, eyes growing. *How could I forget about my luggage?* He opened the closet and pulled a rolling suitcase out. He lay it flat next to Katie's pale feet.

Kasper said, "Perfect. Listen, a few years ago, there was this case in Japan. Workers at a train station found a suitcase abandoned in a coin locker. They took it and kept it in storage for about a month. You know, hoping the owner would come back and claim it. But no one ever came looking. And after that month passed, they opened it and found an elderly woman's body stuffed inside."

Max stuttered, "You–You're saying I should... take her to Japan and leave her in a coin locker?"

"No, you doofus. Put her in the suitcase, take it up to the roof, and leave it there. They'll find it sooner or later, but I don't think they'll open it right away. They won't give you a month, but you'll buy yourself enough time to get out of the country or think of some other way to get out of this."

"Yeah, I guess that sounds better than carrying her out like this. I mean, it *will* work, right?"

"You won't know unless you try. So, start trying."

Max took his folded clothes out of the suitcase and placed the garments on the entertainment center. He removed the luggage tag, which had his name and address on it, then he checked all of the pockets for anything that could link him to the suitcase. It was empty.

He hooked his arms under her armpits and dragged her over the suitcase, then he carefully lowered her upper body into it. She only fit down to her waist. He frowned as he pushed the side of her head until her left ear touched her shoulder. He flinched upon hearing something *pop* in her neck. It only bought him an extra inch of space.

He folded her arms over her breasts, then he crouched over to the other side of the suitcase. He knelt down between her legs. His gaze wandered to her crotch. *Don't look at her privates,* he told himself. *It's wrong, it's disrespectful.* He lifted her legs and propped them up against his shoulders, her pedicured toes pointing at the ceiling. Then he leaned forward and pushed her legs down towards her torso.

Her muscles were relaxed, so she was malleable, but she wasn't a very flexible person. Her body was bent at about a forty-five-degree angle.

He leaned back and said, "She's not going to fit."

"You didn't even try," Kasper said.

"I did."

"Oh, *please*, Max. Don't try pulling that shit on me.

You asked me for my help and I'm giving it to you. Get her into that suitcase or you're fucked."

"I tried, man," Max responded, his voice raspy from all his crying and screaming.

With his elbows on his knees, Kasper leaned forward and said, "*Try. Again.*"

"Goddammit."

Max leaned forward, pushing her legs down towards her torso while throwing all of his weight at her. He heard muffled crunching and crackling sounds coming from her body. His face was about a foot away from hers—and her *feet* were about a foot away from her own face, too. He could *smell* her blood. He could *taste* the coppery flavor at the back of his mouth. He turned away, fighting off the urge to cry.

He managed to flatten her legs against her body—thighs on her abdomen, knees on her breasts. But her legs were longer than her torso. Her feet stuck out from the top of the suitcase. He grabbed her ankles and pushed them down to stop her legs from bouncing back like a spring. He crouched forward, feet around the suitcase, then he sat on her thighs.

He jumped a little upon feeling something wet on the back of his pants. He looked down at her crotch. More dark urine and soft feces oozed out of her. He had her shit and piss on his pants.

"Fuck," he muttered. He glared at Kasper and asked, "Why didn't you warn me?"

"I'm not watching her asshole, buddy," Kasper said, smirking.

Max shook his head. He turned his attention back to the body. He pulled her ankles up towards him, then back down towards her—up-and-over. He pressed her lower legs against her thighs. She looked like a pyramid of human flesh. Fingers splayed out, he held her legs down with one hand as he stood up. Just as he reached over to close the suitcase, Katie's legs unfolded.

"Fuck!" he yelled.

"Keep your voice down."

"I wouldn't be screaming if you'd just help me out a little."

"I'm helping you as much as I can. Believe me, Max, I want you to get out of this just as much as you do."

"Just tell me what to do. How do I make her fit?"

"Well, why don't you try folding her the other way?"

"What good would that do? She's too big, Kasper."

"You don't know that yet. I mean, the way I see it, her legs are flopping out because that's just the way the human body is built. So, if you *break* the human body, you'll have more control over her, right?"

Max said, "I don't know what you're saying. Just spell it out for me already. What am I supposed to do?"

"Fold her the other way. Break her spine and she *might* fit in that suitcase."

Max scratched his hair and looked down at the dead body. He wasn't sure if Kasper was correct, but he didn't have any other ideas anyway. Without taking her out of the suitcase, he rolled her onto her stomach and pushed her legs up, her toes aiming at Kasper. He leaned forward and pushed her legs towards her back.

"It's not working," he said.

"Put your foot on her back and push her legs down," Kasper instructed. "Don't be afraid to break her. She's not going to feel a thing."

Max struggled to his feet while holding her ankles. He stepped on the small of her back, but he hesitated. He caught a glimpse of the fresh feces smeared on her ass and the urine glistening on her genitalia. *What have I done to this poor girl?*—he thought. He breathed in deeply, then he pushed her legs down.

Muffling *crunching* and *popping* sounds came from her pelvis. From the corner of his eye, he saw more feces coming out of her anus like soft-serve ice cream.

"Jesus Christ," he whimpered.

"Just do it already, Max," Kasper said. "Push it."

"She won't fit."

"We've been through this. You won't know unless you try."

"I–I've been trying."

"You're not trying hard enough. Do it, Max. Do it! Put your back into it!"

Kasper's booming voice made Max wince. He had been scolded for screaming, so he didn't expect Kasper to yell at him.

He said, "Ka–Kasper, please don't–"

"Do it!"

"I'm trying! She won't–"

"*Do it!*"

"Damn it, I'm trying my best!"

Max screamed as he pushed her legs down with all of his strength. Her lumbar spine broke with a hair-raising *snap*. Max stumbled off her and crashed into the entertainment center. His eyes expanded with fear, then shrank into a squint of disbelief, then grew again. He couldn't believe it. He had folded her in half, her feet sticking out from the top of the suitcase—heels over her head.

"You did it," Kasper said. "Now close it and get her out of here."

Max couldn't move. He kept hearing the awful *snapping* of her spine echoing through his skull. His blood ran cold. The hairs at the nape of his neck prickled. Tears, as icy as the sweat coating his brow, coursed down his cheeks. He had already killed her, but he believed he was still hurting her. *Desecration*—he was desecrating her corpse and it felt immoral. Questions regarding life and death ran through his mind.

'*Can dead people feel pain?*'

'*Is there an afterlife?*'

'*If souls are real, does she know what I've done?*'

'*Can she see what I'm doing?*'

He whispered, "I'm sorry."

Kasper said, "You don't have time for this. Think about Andrea. Think about your baby. You have to get her out of here. *Now*."

Max let out a trembling sigh as he crawled forward. He closed the luggage over Katie's folded corpse. Her feet stuck out from the top, so he bent her legs at the knees and then tucked her feet into the gaps above her shoulders. And—*voila!*—she was stuffed into the suitcase. The zipper crinkled as it slid, but it came to a stop after five inches.

Max yanked it again. It didn't budge. He tugged on it and leaned back. Yet again, it didn't move. He sat on the suitcase and pulled on the zipper, holding his breath and grinding his teeth.

It moved about a millimeter.

"Damn it," Max gasped. He took a moment to catch his breath, then he said, "You don't have to touch her body, you don't even have to touch the zipper, but can you at least sit on this thing with me? It'll help. I know it will."

"I wish I could, but I can't take a risk like that. They find the smallest thread from my pants on that suitcase and it's game over for us. They might even track me from my lint. Who knows, right?"

"Well, this thing isn't going to close without your help, so what the hell am I supposed to do now?"

"To be honest, I don't think it would close even *with* my help. She's too big."

"That's what I said before!"

"Come on, man, keep it down," Kasper said, raising his hands with his palms down. Max wanted to berate him, but he bit his tongue. Sitting on the luggage, he lowered his head and clenched his jaw. Kasper said, "You're right. You were absolutely right. I'm sorry for pushing you, but we wouldn't have known for sure if you didn't try."

Max asked, "So, what's the plan? You know about other cases like this, don't you? What else can I do?"

Hmm—Kasper hummed with his index finger over his lips as he ran his eyes over the room. He said, "There has to be another way to get this body out of this room... something we haven't thought about yet... I'm sure there's another exit, another way out..." His gaze stopped on the foyer of the room. He could see the bathroom light on the vanity mirror's reflection. A glint of hope in his eyes, he said, "Because there *is* another way out."

5

HUMAN WASTES

MAX AND KASPER STOOD IN THE BATHROOM DOORWAY and stared at the toilet. The light above the mirror hummed incessantly. Water dripped from the leaky sink faucet, *plopping* every few seconds.

Kasper said, "A guy in Mexico—he was drunk or drugged or both, I don't really remember—he killed his girlfriend after an argument about drinking. And he's... he's out of his mind, okay? He is fucked up *and* he fucked up big time, you know what I'm saying? So, what does he do? He starts *skinning* her and *flushing* her down the toilet. He flushed some of her organs down, too, so it wasn't just her skin."

Arms crossed, sneering in disgust, Max responded, "But he didn't get away with it, did he? You know about it because he got caught, right?"

"That is true, my friend, *but* listen to what I'm saying. *He* was fucked up. You're not drunk, are you?"

Max shook his head.

Kasper asked, "Are you high?"

Max shook his head again.

Kasper said, "So, you have a better chance at making this work than he ever did. You know what a toilet can handle. You can chop her up into the tiniest pieces and flush her down."

"Okay, maybe... maybe that can work, but what about her bones, Kasper? Those won't go down without bursting a pipe. And if I cause any damage, they'll know where to start looking."

"Then don't flush the big bones. Just cut her down until she fits in the suitcase. Then give the bones to some stray dogs or bury 'em in the woods. Simple, right?'

Max gazed into Kasper's bright, eager eyes. They shared many morbid interests: Serial killers, mass shooters, human experimentation, politics. But Kasper had always had a stronger stomach for the grotesque nature of mankind. He understood the difference between life and death, but he also recognized their connection.

A person could not be alive without having to die, and a person could not die without having lived.

Max sighed as he walked back to the bedroom. He stood over the suitcase, eyes on Katie's cold, pale feet.

He asked, "Are you sure there isn't any other way?"

Kasper approached him from behind and said, "The toilet is the only other exit from this room. You can try to roll her out of here in that suitcase like that, but someone's going to notice those feet."

"Couldn't I just cut off her feet?"

"Then what? Keep the pieces in your luggage so the blood can leak out?"

"Shit," Max muttered. "Okay. Then couldn't we... hire someone? You know, someone to take care of this for us?"

Kasper chuckled, then he said, "First of all, I think you meant to say, 'take care of this for *me.*' As in, *you,* Max, because I had nothing to do with this. Secondly... *who?* Who are you going to hire to help you with something like this? The fucking mob?"

"Come on, man, you know what I mean. There has to be some sort of... dead body disposal service or something like that on the deep web, right? You said, 'money can make all of your problems go away.' You said that earlier, didn't you? So, it–it has to be possible. There has to be *someone* who can do this."

"Even if a service like that existed—and it probably only exists for millionaires and politicians—I wouldn't know where to start looking. Do you even know how to access the deep web? Are you even sure something like that would be available here? Remember, Maxie, time is of the essence."

"Shit," Max sighed. "You're right."

He crouched in front of the suitcase and opened it. He turned Katie's head until he could see her bruised face. His sneer grew larger as he examined her injuries.

He asked, "What if we set it up to look like a suicide or an accident?"

"I'm listening."

"I could... I could roll her over to the stairs in this suitcase. Just like this, right? Then I just... I throw her down the stairs. I wait a few minutes, then I act like I found her like this. That could work, right?"

"Max," Kasper said before pausing dramatically. He exhaled loudly, then he said, "It won't work. Look at her, man. Her face is completely swollen. Her spine is broken. You would have to push her down every flight of stairs in this building to make it look believable. Besides, if you report her body, the investigation will begin immediately. That means they're going to be looking at surveillance footage. They'll see you and they'll connect everything. You don't want them to start looking so soon. Remember, you *need* to buy time. That's what this is all about."

"Damn it, I really don't have a choice, do I?" Max said. He caressed Katie's hair and whispered, "I'm sorry."

"You should go out and buy some tools to chop her up."

'*Buy some tools to chop her up.*' Max covered his face and sniveled upon hearing those words. Those words didn't sound pleasant in any context, but they were talking about a young woman. It was atrocious. He looked up at the ceiling, hoping gravity would help him keep his tears in his eyes.

Kasper said, "Seriously, you can't do this with your hands."

Max responded, "She had a knife in her bag. I–I'll use that."

"You should buy a hacksaw."

"Shut up."

"I'm just saying, it would go a lot easier if you bought some sort of saw or a butcher–"

"Shut up!" Max yelled as he sprung to his feet.

Kasper raised his hands and stepped back towards the front door. He could see he was getting under Max's skin. But Max didn't detect any fear in his eyes or posture. *Why aren't you scared of me?*—he wanted to ask. It all rubbed him the wrong way.

Max said, "I'll use her knife. I don't want to go out there right now. It's too risky. Let's just try the toilet. Will you help me out?"

Kasper didn't answer, but his silence spoke volumes for him. Max pressed his tongue against the side of his mouth and nodded—'*Thought so.*' He grabbed the suitcase's handle and dragged the luggage into the bathroom, then he went back into the bedroom and unwrapped the bedsheets. He took the switchblade out of Katie's purse.

A 3.5-inch blade snapped out of the handle with the press of a button. He shuddered upon seeing his reflection on the blade. He didn't recognize himself.

He went back to the bathroom and placed the knife on the counter. Then he crouched and unfolded Katie. He rolled her onto her back without taking her torso out of the suitcase.

Just as Max grabbed the knife, Kasper said, "Wait." Max glanced back at him. Kasper said, "Take off your shirt."

"Huh?"

"Your shirt. You don't want to get more of her blood on it right now. You can hide a few drops, sure, but you can't walk out of here looking like you took a bath in her blood, right?"

Max set the knife down and walked out of the bathroom. He removed his button-up shirt and wife beater in front of the vanity mirror, then he folded his clothes and put them on the entertainment center. He stopped on his way back to the bathroom. He was a fit man. He wasn't a model with rippling abs and bulging muscles, but he was healthy.

But he—like most people—had a tendency to focus on his flaws. His pecs were a little loose and his stomach was flabby. He could work on his triceps, too.

"Max," Kasper said. His voice grabbed Max's attention. Kasper asked, "Shouldn't you think about taking your pants off, too?"

"I think it'll be fine. They're dark, so no one will notice a little bit of blood."

"But better safe than sorry, no?"

"It would be better if you helped me, *no?*"

Kasper nodded, bit his bottom lip, and raised his hands again, as if to say: *Sorry, sorry, didn't mean to offend you.*

He asked, "So, you ready to get started?"

"No," Max said. "But I have no choice."

Max crouched beside the suitcase. He looked Katie over from head to toe, his eyes filled with reluctance. He pressed the blade against her belly button as he considered disemboweling her first. Images of bloody intestines flashed in his mind, causing him to shut his eyes and shake his head. *Too grotesque,* he thought. He tapped the blade on her prominent ribs, as if he were playing a xylophone. He pictured himself trying to snap her ribs out of her chest, then peeling the flesh off them. *Too difficult,* he thought, shaking his head in disappointment.

Leaning against the doorway, arms and legs crossed, Kasper asked, "Did you have sex with her?"

"What kind of question is that?" Max responded without taking his eyes off the corpse.

"An important one."

"Why?"

"The answer will give you a starting point. It'll make it easier for you to decide where to begin, you know?"

Max looked up at him and asked, "What do you mean by that?"

"If you fucked her, start with her pelvis. I don't know how to say this in a... a 'respectful' way but... but cut her pussy out. Tear her uterus out. Rip it *all* out. Especially if you didn't use a condom and you cummed inside of her. That evidence is the most damning. Get rid of it, okay?"

Shocked by Kasper's horrendous speech, Max stammered, "I–I–I didn't fuck her."

"Good. So, you should–"

"But she sucked my dick. I didn't cum, but she... Yeah, she sucked my dick. And she cut it a little. I mean, she bit it because I hit her. It's not too bad, I don't need to go to the hospital or anything like that, but... it's cut and it bled."

Kasper said, "Damn, dude. So, here's what *I* think you should do: Start with her mouth. Cut her tongue out, as much of it as possible, then pull her teeth out. By severing her tongue, you increase your chances of hiding your DNA. By taking her teeth, you'll make it harder for the police to identify her. All of that should flush down the toilet easily, too."

Max nodded and crouched over to the top of the suitcase. He placed his palm against her forehead to hold her down.

Kasper said, "Just grab her hair. It'll be easier for you. Besides, you're going to have to scalp her later anyway."

"Damn it," Max sighed.

He took a minute to breathe, each breath shakier than the last. He grabbed a fistful of Katie's hair and pushed her head down. He heard a crinkling sound. He couldn't tell if it came from the blood crusted on her hair or if his grip was so tight that he was tearing the locks off her scalp.

Max rubbed the tip of the blade on her swollen lips. He wiggled it to pry her mouth open. The blade nicked her upper lip. A droplet of blood dribbled out towards her crushed nostril. Then the tip of the blade *clinked* against her chipped teeth. He twirled his wrist and stirred the knife in her mouth. It cut her bottom lip in half vertically down the middle, then it sliced her gums, then it cut her upper lip again. He couldn't get it to slip past her teeth. Fresh blood crawled across her face.

While trying to force the knife into her mouth, Max kept glancing at her eyes, expecting them to pop open or twitch from the pain. It was a strange experience to hurt someone's body without actually hurting that person. Pain was built entirely in the brain, and it was difficult to accept that for some people.

Kasper said, "Maxie... Maxie... *Max*." Max finally stopped twisting the knife in her mouth. Kasper said, "It's probably the rigor mortis. It starts with the smaller muscles, like those in the face. Cut her cheeks open, then try pulling her jaw down."

Max smiled nervously, obviously fighting off tears, and said, "It's easier said than done."

"This was never going to be easy, bud."

"Ahh, shit..."

Max swallowed loudly, snorting as he breathed through his nose. He slid the knife into her oral vestibule—the gap between her teeth and cheek. Then he tilted it to the side, away from her face. The blade cut into the edge of her lips, then he sawed through her cheek. The tip of the blade *clinked* against her teeth each time, scraping away at her enamel. One of her molars, already damaged during the beating, broke in half—bloody pulp sticking out of it.

He sawed until he reached the ramus of her mandible—her jawbone under her left ear. He could see her bloodied teeth through the thin slit on her cheek.

He shoved the knife into the opposite oral vestibule and started sawing. The sound of her cheek tearing—a moist crinkling sound—made him cringe. The knife shook in his hand, leaving a jagged cut on her face. Yet again, he stopped as the blade scraped her mandible. He hadn't realized it until he was done, but he had carved a smile onto her face, cuts curving up towards her ears. Blood from her facial wounds cascaded down her jaw and spilled onto her neck. It painted the bottom half of her face red.

"What am I doing?" Max whispered as he stared at his bloody fingertips.

"Don't stop to think about it," Kasper said. "Just do it."

"I'm a monster."

"Max, you either flush her down the toilet and say goodbye to her body... or you say goodbye to your family and your life. *Don't think about it.*"

"I'm a monster," Max repeated, his voice shaking.

He was haunted by guilt. It festered in his heart and rotted his mind. It twisted his intestines over his other organs, crushing them with the grip of a boa constrictor. A knot of nausea surfaced in his stomach. He needed another moment to recompose himself, so he washed his hands with hot water in the bathtub.

In a calm, understanding tone, Kasper said, "I don't

mean to pressure you, but I can't stick around if you're not going to give this your all."

"I–I'm doing it. I just needed a second. But I *will* do it."

"You *have* to do it, Maxie. You have no choice."

Max set the knife down on the tile floor. He grabbed a fistful of Katie's hair in one hand and gripped her jaw in the other, immediately bloodying his hands again. With disappointment written on his face, he moved his hands in opposite directions. Crinkling and popping sounds came from the corpse's head as her mouth slowly opened.

"God," Max muttered, frowning.

A wet crackling sound came out of Katie's mouth —*a death rattle*. It was the most disturbing sound he had ever heard.

He thrust the knife into her mouth at a downward angle, skewering her tongue. He weaved and bobbed his head, trying to get a better view around the blade, but to no avail. So, he jerked the knife in every direction—up and down, left and right, diagonally that way and diagonally this way. He leaned forward and nearly lost his balance as the blade slid out of her tongue.

It severed her uvula and cut her oropharynx—the back of her mouth. Her uvula was mashed into her throat. Her soft palate and tonsils were cut as he twisted the knife. He managed to stab her tongue again. He grabbed the switchblade's handle in the icepick grip and moved it in all directions again, like a joystick at an arcade.

After about a minute, he successfully cut her tongue in half. It wasn't a clean cut, but he got the job done. He grabbed it and—as if it were fresh off a hot stove—he tossed it at the toilet quickly. It hit the lid with a *splat*, then it plunged into the bowl and landed in the water with a *plop*.

"Flush it," Kasper demanded.

Max crawled over to the toilet. He touched the handle and gazed into the bowl, watching as plumes of dark blood undulated away from the sinking tongue. A few hours ago, that tongue—that bloody, mutilated tongue—was a source of great sexual pleasure. Now, it was equivalent to a piece of shit from someone suffering from rectal bleeding.

Kasper repeated, "*Flush it.*"

Max pushed the handle down. The tongue went down the toilet without a problem. Clean water filled the bowl again.

"Do her teeth next," Kasper said coldly. He didn't seem bothered by the gore. He said, "Would be easier if you had a wrench or a hammer, but I guess you can stab 'em until they pop out."

Kasper's apathy didn't sound the alarms in Max's head. He could only nod as he stared at the toilet water. He crouched back to the other side of the suitcase. He pushed her upper lip up with his index finger and her bottom lip down with his thumb. He drew another deep breath, then he thrust the blade at her teeth, like someone breaking ice with an icepick. Some of her incisor teeth crumbled, enamel falling on the mushy pulp accumulating at the back of her mouth.

He adjusted his aim and started *peeling* her upper gums with the blade. Shavings of her flesh spiraled down to the back of her mouth, joining her severed uvula and broken teeth. He shaved her gums until he could see the roots of her teeth. He repeated the process on her lower gums, grinding the blade against the tender tissue. The knife even scraped her teeth, screeching like a metal rake on concrete.

He folded the knife, then he struck her teeth with the butt of the switchblade. He hammered away at her mouth until her teeth fell out of her butchered gums. Some of them shattered during the beating. Her incisors and canines landed on the base of her tongue. He hooked his index and middle fingers over her bottom lip and gums to pry her jaw open. He grimaced upon feeling her gummy flesh. It reminded him of an elderly person's toothless mouth.

He drew the blade, then he thrust it at her gums, burying it under a molar. He flicked the blade up, forcing the tooth to pop out. Using the same method, he plucked the rest of her teeth out one by one. Then he moved her head to the side and shook it until all of her loose teeth fell out of her mouth, like a child trying to get his coins out of a piggy bank. He grabbed the pieces from the luggage and dumped them in the toilet. Some pieces made bigger splashes than others.

Plop, plop, PLOP, plop, PLOP!

Hand on the handle, he paused to watch the clouds

of blood billowing away from the teeth. He sighed so loud that the water rippled because of his breath. He flushed the toilet. The teeth clinked against the bowl before going down the drain.

"Now do her fingers," Kasper said. "Maybe her toes after."

Max crouched his way back to the suitcase, eyes dim and watery. From his periphery, he could see her carved up mouth. He washed his hands in the bathtub, then he grabbed a wad of toilet paper and placed it over her mutilated cheek. He took her right arm out of the luggage. It was stiff. *Rigor mortis,* he thought. He splayed her fingers out and slapped her palm on the tile floor.

He held the blade over the base of her fingers. She had small hands, but he didn't want to take any unnecessary risks. He had seen toilets clog with smaller feces and thinner toilet paper. He moved the blade to the joints at the center of her fingers. *Still too big,* he thought. The blade gravitated to the joints closest to her fingertips.

Perfect.

He sawed into her index finger. The joint crunched and cracked. It took him thirty seconds to sever it. A weak column of blood shot out of it. He cut into the joint at the center of her finger next, then he sawed into the knuckle at the base of it. The *crunch* from that knuckle was the loudest. A piece of her bone splintered out of her hand.

Sniffling and whimpering, he chopped up all of her

fingers in the same way, severing each phalange. He refused to stop because he knew he wouldn't be able to start again if he did. He threw the fingers into the bowl and flushed the toilet. He was relieved to see them go down without a problem but sickened and saddened by his own actions.

He took her other arm out of the luggage, slapped her palm on the floor, and stretched her fingers out. Then he mangled her hand. He amputated her fingers —one by one, *joint* by *joint*. Sweat glistened on his neck and chest. Blood spewed from her fingers and soaked his hands. It ran down the grooves between the tiles, too.

The cannibals in the movies made it look easy, like chopping vegetables for dinner.

He threw the pieces into the toilet and quickly flushed it, then he washed his hands in the bathtub. Thin streams of bloody water shimmered in the tub. He turned his attention to the dead body. Fingerless hands were common in cartoons and comics, but the commonality of humans often led to dysmorphophobia when disfigurements were present in real life. People were supposed to have five fingers on each hand, so it was jarring for Max to see someone with none.

He closed his eyes, held his clenched fist over his lips, and he swallowed until his mouth was dry. A tear from his left eye trickled down to his stubble. A thick goop of mucus dripped from his nostril. He rushed to the sink and turned the faucet on. He splashed water on his face, then he drank some from his cupped hands, and then he splashed more water on his face. He turned the faucet off and stared at himself in the mirror, his entire body moving with each heavy breath.

As red as rubies, his eyes were bloodshot from his excessive crying. He pulled his lower eyelid down. He couldn't see a slit of white in his sclera. Sweat stood out on his forehead, black pouches of flesh hung under his eyes, and an alarming pallor surrounded his flushed cheeks. He looked dead. The stress and guilt had taken a toll on his physical and mental health. He clenched his jaw and fists. He sought self-punishment as a form of redemption, but he fought off his desire to strike the mirror.

Escape and survival were his primary concerns. Self-punishment could wait until he got away from the crime scene without handcuffs around his wrists.

He unfurled his fists and sighed, then he asked, "What's next?"

No one answered.

"Her feet? No, her... her toes, right?" he asked. "Isn't that what you said?"

Once again, there was no response.

He glanced over at the doorway. Kasper was gone. He looked behind him. Katie was still in the suitcase.

He said, "Kasper? Kasper, what are you doing?"

He squinted and cocked his head to the side upon hearing a muffled voice in the bedroom. He didn't recognize it. Then his eyes widened in alarm. A horrifying possibility crept into his mind: *He's talking to the police, he's selling me out.*

As he hurried out of the bathroom, Max shouted, "Kasper! *John!*"

He crashed into the closet door, then he lurched into the bedroom. The TV wobbled as he bumped into the entertainment center. He came to a sudden stop at the foot of the bed. He found Kasper standing next to the nightstand, his arms crossed and his brow raised.

"What are you doing, Maxie?" Kasper asked.

Max pointed the switchblade at him and said, "Don't you dare try to turn this on me. What were *you* doing?"

"What are you talking about? I was just standing here. Getting some fresh air, you know?"

"You were talking to someone!" Max snapped at him while taking a step towards him.

Kasper huffed, then he said, "Put the knife down, man."

"Did you call the cops?"

"What? *No.* No, I didn't call the fucking cops."

Max took another step towards him. Kasper raised his hand at him and stepped back, as if he were stepping away from a feral animal.

"I don't know what you heard, but I know what I was doing," Kasper said. "I stepped out after you flushed her fingers down the toilet. I needed to catch my breath. It was... It was getting intense. And I could... smell the blood. I couldn't handle it. I knew you needed a break, too. I definitely wasn't calling the cops. I mean, did you see me with a phone in my hand? Are you even sure you heard *my* voice?"

Max stopped after taking a third step. *He's right,* he thought. *I can't be sure that I heard his voice. Maybe it was someone else. Maybe it was nothing.* He lowered the knife, face twisted with confusion.

Kasper breathed a sigh of relief. He said, "It's fine to be scared, but you really need to relax. You can't be running at me with a knife, Maxie. I'm here to help you. I'm risking my freedom, my life, for *you*. We're supposed to be in this together. Don't let the stress get to your head, my man. It'll make you see things—*hear things*—that aren't actually there. That's when the mistakes start happening."

"You–You're right. I'm just scared—stupid and scared. I think I'm..."

'*I think I'm losing my mind.*' He couldn't say those words to him. He was already a murderer. He didn't want Kasper to see him as homicidal *and* unstable.

He said, "I'm just sorry that I dragged you into this."

"And I'm sorry for stepping out without saying anything. I shouldn't have done that. But hey, let's look at the bright side: It's working. Our plan is actually working. As long as you keep your head in the game, you're going to get out of this. So, what do you say? You want to finish up now? Are you ready?"

"Ye–Yeah. Yeah, let's finish this."

The men returned to the bathroom. Kasper stayed in the doorway and Max crouched beside the suitcase.

Kasper said, "If her fingers went down without a problem, then we don't have to worry about the toes right now. They're smaller, so they'll go down without clogging the toilet. Let's step it up a little. Why don't you try cutting off her tits?"

"Her... tits?"

"Yeah, I mean, they're not so big, are they? Maybe C or even B-cups, right?"

Max poked her right nipple with the blade. He moved the knife to her sternum, then up to her collarbone.

He said, "Um... So... Where should I start?"

Kasper shrugged and said, "Anywhere, I guess. Maybe from the bottom, then go all around it?"

Max pressed the tip of the blade against the fold at the bottom of her breast—the inframammary ridge. He squeezed her breast in his other hand, her puffy nipple rubbing up against his palm. His grip was only supposed to make it easier for him to sever her breast, but he felt like he was groping her. He trembled and whined, disgusted with himself.

He thrust the blade upward into her breast. Blood leaked out, lining the fold under her tit. He sawed into it, dragging the blade towards her sternum, then up towards her clavicle. Blood puddled on her cleavage, splattered on both her breasts, and cascaded down her stomach. The blood from her breast connected to the blood on her neck, which came from her mutilated face.

Up and over, Max sawed to the left, moving the

blade towards her armpit. After about five minutes, he reached the initial incision at the bottom of her breast. He tightened his grip on her tit and pulled it up towards himself. He heard a wet crackling sound. He tugged on it again, but it wouldn't budge. He leaned in towards her stomach and peeked into the gash.

Through the slimy blood, he saw layers of yellow fat, the clusters of lobules and the tubular lacteal ducts, and her torn ligaments. The fat oozed out from the side of her breast, thick like cottage cheese. Her breast was still attached to her pectoral muscle. To Max, it all looked like bloody ground beef.

He thrust the blade back into the gash while continuing to pull on her breast. He whimpered and gagged as his thumb brushed up against her lobules. He held his breath and accelerated his thrusting, stabbing the inside of her tit as quickly as possible. He fell back and crashed into the sink cabinet with her amputated breast in his hand as he finally severed it.

"Je–Jesus," he croaked out as he gaped at the bloody breast. His eyes, already appearing too big for their sockets, grew larger as he looked at the huge, circular wound on the corpse's chest. He cried, *"What the fuck?!"*

"Flush it," Kasper said. "Don't look at her, don't think about it. Just flush it, Max. Come on, you can do this."

Max looked up at his friend. Kasper's presence was reassuring and his words were motivational. *You can do this,* he thought. *I can do this.* He crawled over Katie's body, threw the tit into the bowl, then he flushed the toilet.

Clunk!

The dull sound came from the toilet. Katie's breast wasn't visible in the bowl, but it was stuck in the pipe. Severed ducts and lobules floated in the bloody water.

"No, no, no," Max whispered. "It's clogging. It's clogged. It's fucking clogged, Kasper!"

"Don't panic. All we need is–"

Max tried to flush the toilet again. The water rose a bit before another *clunk* echoed through the hotel room.

Kasper said, "Max, stop it." Max flushed the toilet a third time. Kasper yelled, "Max!"

"It's not working, man!"

"Because you keep flushing! Stop it! We only need to get a plunger and–"

A fourth time.

Max pushed down on the handle for the *fourth* time. The bloody water overflowed and cascaded across the bowl. It pooled around the toilet.

Kasper grabbed his shoulders, pulled him up to his feet, and shook him. Max could see Kasper's lips flapping and the anger in his eyes, but he couldn't hear a thing.

Max stuttered, "I–I don't know wha–what you're saying. I don't... I–I don't..." He swayed back and forth, dizzy and weak. He whispered, "I don't know what I'm doing."

Then he fainted.

6

A NIGHTMARE OF A DREAM

"What am I doing here?" Max asked in a hushed voice.

He stood in his bedroom, a kitchen knife in his right hand. He wore flannel pajamas and slippers—his regular sleepwear. Moonlight pierced the blinds over the window behind him. And the window overlooked the city's glamorous skyline. The apartment was silent, not a creak from the floorboards or a groan from the pipes.

Andrea, his fiancé, slept on her back on the bed in front of him, hands on her firm belly. She was 24 weeks pregnant.

Max moved her arms to her sides, then he pulled the blanket down to her thighs. He stopped and stared at her smooth, babyish face—still sleeping. He pushed her nightgown up to her breasts. The waistband of her stretchy black panties sat beneath her baby bump. He stood there in the dark, eyes fixed on her stomach.

Five minutes passed.

Then ten minutes.

Then fifteen.

Andrea put her left hand on her belly, snuggled her face against her pillow, and adjusted her legs. She fell into a deeper slumber, unaware of Max's presence next to her.

"Do it," a male voice, soft and raspy, whispered.

Max looked at the window. There was no one behind him. He glanced at the floor lamp in the corner to his left, then at the closet door beside the nightstand to his right.

"Did I say that?" Max murmured.

He turned his attention to Andrea. The voices didn't bother her. He moved her arm to her side again, then he rubbed the blade against her belly. It glided effortlessly. Andrea curled her lip as she swiped at the knife. She scratched her stomach, then she rested her hand on her belly. The cold stainless-steel blade had irritated her.

Max waited for a minute before moving her arm again. He slid the tip of the blade into her belly button, then he twirled the knife around, as if he were screwing a nail with a screwdriver. He sniffled while licking his dry lips. He flicked tears off his eyelashes with each blink. His face twitched and his hand trembled.

The blade nicked her belly button. A thread of blood ran down the side of her belly. But she didn't awaken.

"Do it," the voice said.

Wiping his face with his sleeve, Max turned around in a circle. There was no one in the room. He assumed he was hearing someone outside, but their apartment was on the 21st floor of the building and the window was closed. It didn't make any sense.

"Do it," the voice repeated—clearer, louder, *angrier*. It wasn't a request. It was a demand.

Max looked at the ceiling and asked, "Do what?"

"Do it."

He turned around in a circle again, teetering with each step. He felt the room spinning and the floor shaking. He stopped while facing the bed, rubbing his eyes with his thumb and index finger.

The voice said, "Do it."

Max muttered indistinctly to himself. The voice sounded familiar. *Is it me? Is it my voice? Am I talking out loud?*—he thought. His mind hunted for a logical explanation, but he couldn't find it. He was convinced the voice was coming from somewhere else.

"Do it," the voice said for the sixth time.

"Ka... Kasper?" Max said with a hint of doubt in his voice. "Is that you?"

"Do it," a woman said.

Max glared at Andrea. She adjusted her pillow, slid her hand under it, then smacked her lips. Her eyes remained closed.

"What did you say?" Max hissed through his gritted teeth. Andrea did not awaken. Max poked her stomach gently with the knife and asked, "Is that what you want me to do? Hmm? Then say it again and I'll do it. I swear I'll really do it."

Andrea stayed asleep. The apartment was quiet. The streets outside were peaceful. But Max's head started to tremble violently, as if it were about to burst open. He ground his teeth, foamy saliva spurting out of his mouth with each exhale. His mind was a battlefield, voices fighting over control of his body. The same phrase kept repeating in his head: *'Do it, do it, do it, do it, do it!'*

"Do it," Andrea said.

Max didn't notice her lips open, but he was positive it was her voice. He turned the knife and held it with the blade pointing downward. He raised it over his shoulder, then he thrust it down at her stomach, stabbing her directly through her belly button and burying the blade in her uterus.

"*Ow!*" Andrea shrieked, jolted awake by the stabbing.

She instinctively reached for the knife, but she writhed in pain before she could touch it. She started hyperventilating. Head swaying in every direction, she couldn't see anything in the dark. She only felt the fierce stinging pain in her abdomen. Her stomach was on fire, pulses of pain reverberating through her torso.

Max pulled the knife out and raised it over his shoulder. Blood dripped from the tip of the blade and plopped on his slippers. It upset him to hear her cries, but he was out of control. Before he knew it, he was thrusting the knife down at her belly again. The blade punctured her placenta, mutilating her intervillous space. Her maternal blood spilled out in waves.

Andrea, sobbing hysterically, slapped her hands over her stomach as the knife slid out of her. She rocked from side to side, blood erupting from her wounds.

"Help! Help!" she cried.

Max kept stabbing her. With the third stab, the knife impaled her hand, shattering two of her metacarpal bones while the tip of the blade cut into her abdomen. The fourth stab cut her lower abdomen, penetrating her uterus and amniotic sac. Amniotic fluid and blood squirted out of her as he removed the knife. The fifth stab severed her left index finger.

The sixth and seventh stabs cut into her abdomen and pierced her uterus. The eighth skewered her right hand straight through the center. A piece of her broken metacarpal bone came out of her palm. As she crossed her arms over her stomach, he stabbed her left forearm two times. Then he drove the blade into her lower abdomen.

With the blade inside of her, Andrea rolled onto her side in a desperate attempt to save herself. Although she didn't realize it at that moment, she had helped Max cut her open. The blade traveled from the center of her abdomen to her left hip—a deep, grisly five-inch gash. On her side, she dragged herself towards the other edge of the bed.

Her cell phone was charging on the desk at the other end of the room. Something inside of her—perhaps her survival instincts—told her she could save herself if she reached it.

"He–He–Help me," she said weakly.

As he climbed onto the bed, Max said, "I'm sorry, baby. I'm so sorry. He told me to do it. You–You told me to–to do it. I can't stop it. I want to but I can't!"

He sat on top of her legs and started stabbing the side of her abdomen. Streaks of blood hit the headboard, the wall, the ceiling, and his face and shirt. His hands and sleeves were soaked in it. The pale-yellow amniotic fluid glistened in the moonlight. Due to the pain and fear, she unintentionally urinated. The piss joined the blood on the bed.

"Stop... stop... Please stop," she begged as she swung her arm at him.

She hit his chest two times and his neck once, but she couldn't hurt him or push him away. And she hadn't yet realized her own fiancé was stabbing her in their bedroom.

Max stabbed her *twenty-three* times before stopping. Some of the gashes were so deep and wide he could see *inside* of her. She gasped for air and then grunted—gasp, grunt, gasp, grunt, *gasp, grunt*. Max could see the pain on her face. The pain broke her physically, mentally, and emotionally. It pushed her into a whole different state of mind, that place between consciousness and unconsciousness.

"I'm sorry, Andrea," Max said in a frail voice.

"Please forgive me. I didn't want to do this, but he won't let me stop. I can't get his damn voice out of my head. It won't leave me alone until I *do it*."

Max rolled Andrea onto her back. He scooted back until he was sitting on her knees. Andrea's head swayed on a pillow, her short hair drenched in sweat. Max stabbed her over her right hip. He sawed into her until he connected the horizontal gashes on her lower abdomen. It was now one long, slanted ten-inch laceration.

He placed the knife on the pillow beside Andrea. Using both hands, he forced his fingers into the cut, then he moved his arms in opposite directions—up towards her torso and down towards her legs. Her abdominal muscles tore as the wound widened. He could see her bloody uterus. He kept one hand inside of her, using his fingers like surgical retractors, and he picked up the knife with the other.

He sawed into her uterus. Her uterus and amniotic sac were torn open. She closed her eyes and panted. Her lips moved as if she were trying to say something, but only croaks and whimpers came out. She swung her arm at him. She hit his elbow with her forearm.

Max said, "Stop it. Don't make this worse for us."

Although it was dark, he could see into the uterus. He saw the lifeless fetus inside of her. He tugged on it, but it was attached to the placenta. So, while pulling on the fetus, he forced the blade back inside of her and sawed away at the umbilical cord until he severed it.

He leaned back, barely keeping his balance as the unborn baby slid out.

As he stared at the fetus, he stuttered, "You–You... You're... You–You're..."

'*You're my kid.*' Those words were true, but shock robbed him of his voice. At heart, he knew it was better if he didn't admit it anyway. He was ashamed of his actions. He brutalized the love of his life and killed his own child before she even had the chance to live.

"Why?!" Max sobbed. "Why am I like this?!"

He cradled the bloody fetus against his chest. It was about ten inches long and it weighed a little more than a pound. It had already developed a humanoid figure—arms, legs, an erect head. Under the blood, the fetus' skin was pink, purple, and red. He could see it was a girl, too.

"Finish it," the male voice said.

Max looked at Andrea. He could see she was still alive. He had killed their child, but he hadn't completed his task. Murder was on his mind and it refused to leave until he killed a conscious person. For him, it didn't count if it wasn't born yet.

"Sh–She's almost dead," Max said. "She'll die on her–"

"Finish it," the voice interrupted.

"She's already dead... She's already dead..."

"Kill her. Kill them all."

"She's already dead!" Max barked at the ceiling. "They're already dead, damn it! Leave me alone!"

"Kill them all!"

The voice was louder and deeper than ever before. It echoed through the building. Like a powerful gust of wind, it even moved the picture frames on the hallway walls.

Max couldn't ignore the demand. He mounted Andrea's waist. He hooked his fingers over her lower teeth and pulled her jaw down, prying her mouth open. Head-first, he shoved the fetus into Andrea's mouth. Her teeth scalped the bald fetus. The fetus' brain popped out of its soft spot like pus from a pimple and hit her uvula, forcing her to gag and shut her mouth.

The infant's body was crushed. Its skull collapsed with more of its brain oozing out from the top of its head. Andrea's taste buds buzzed, overwhelmed by the pungent flavor of blood. She didn't realize her dead baby was stuffed in her mouth.

And Max kept pushing it. The fetus' crushed head slid into her throat, causing a thick lump to protrude from her neck. The fetus' tiny feet stuck out from her mouth. Its legs were so thin, so malleable, that they could have fit in the narrow gaps between Andrea's teeth.

Frothy blood spumed out of Andrea's mouth around the dead fetus. Her eyes rolled as she convulsed under Max. After about a minute, she stopped moving.

"It's done, it–it's finished," Max said, frowning and sniveling.

Max sat there in silence. He looked over at the floor

lamp in the corner of the room, then at the window, and then at the ceiling.

He said, "Hello? Can you hear me? Is... Is anyone there?"

The voice was gone.

7

PLAN C

Max awoke bolt-upright on a bed, cold sweat dripping from his face. He looked at his bloody hands, then at the opposite side of the bed. Andrea and the fetus were nowhere in sight. His gaze drifted up until he saw the sitting area at the end of the room. He looked straight ahead and found the entertainment center. And to his right, he found Kasper.

"You were dreaming," Kasper said. "Well, judging from the things you were saying and the way you were moving, I would guess you were having a nightmare. 'Nightmaring?' Is that a word?"

Max stuttered, "Wha–What are you talking about? I was... You're saying I was... dreaming? *That* was a dream?"

"I don't know what 'that' is, Maxie. I wasn't dreaming with you, you know, but yeah, I think you were having a dream. Do you remember anything?"

"A–About my dream?"

"I meant before that."

Max shook his head.

Kasper said, "But you remember, um..." He leaned closer to him and, as if he were afraid someone would hear him, he whispered, "You remember killing that girl in the bathroom, don't you?"

Max nodded.

Kasper said, "Good, good. I was worried you might have forgotten it all. Anyway, you, uh... you tried flushing her tit down the toilet. You panicked and you clogged it. The toilet overflowed a little, but it's nothing you can't clean up with a couple of towels. You fell unconscious. You woke up for a minute and tried to leave the room. I didn't let you. Then you came here and went to bed. You were asleep for thirty, maybe forty-five minutes."

"Thirty minutes?" Max repeated in an uncertain tone. "No, it... it must have been an hour or two. I was watching her for..."

He stopped before he could recount his nightmare. Although he was already a killer, he didn't want to scare Kasper off with his visions of murder. One murder could be excused as an accident—a mistake or a heat-of-the-moment type of thing—two murders in a short period of time could be considered a spree killing, and three or more murders made the culprit a serial killer. He needed Kasper to believe Katie's death was an accident.

Kasper asked, "Watching who? What were you dreaming about?"

"It's nothing. Never mind."

Kasper smiled and said, "Come on, man, you can't just leave me hanging like that. What was it? If it was about this whole mess, you know I won't judge. This is a scary situation, Max. It's normal to be terrified and traumatized."

"Okay, look, I was just... I guess I was having a nightmare of a dream."

"*Huh?*"

"It was a nightmare of... of something that I always wanted to do. A nightmare of a dream, an aspiration, a–a hope, a... a goal."

Kasper puckered his lips and nodded, then he repeated, "A nightmare of a dream... That's an interesting way to put it."

Max dreamt of bloody murder. He had an untamable desire to kill a person. As a teenager, he thought about murdering his classmates. As a college student, he contemplated killing a homeless man. Now, he was obsessed with murdering his fiancé. He had hoped killing a prostitute would make the urges go away, but the nightmares kept haunting his sleep.

Staring down at himself, he said, "I'm sick."

"I know," Kasper responded. "But you'll have to deal with that later. The girl in the bathroom, she's your priority now."

Max sniffled, then he covered his mouth with his hand. His eyes welled with tears and his head ached. He could smell Katie's dead body—the blood, the urine, the feces—from the bedroom.

He said, "It's fucked up. Nothing's working. What am I supposed to do now? What the hell am I–"

"Calm down," Kasper interrupted as he sat at the foot of the bed. "You can't overreact. You can't throw another tantrum like you did in the bathroom. That could have got you busted. And it just wasted your precious time. So, let's stop all the screaming and crying. Let's focus on getting rid of that dead body. Okay?"

"Ye–Yeah, you're right. I just don't know what to do. She's not going down that toilet. Even if I unclog it, it's just going to clog again. And if someone notices the flushing, it's all over. And she's bloodier than before. I can't just drag her out of here. I mean, she's... she's missing one of her breasts for crying out loud."

Kasper said, "You're absolutely right, Max. While you were out cold, I was... brainstorming. I came up with an idea. Let's call it 'Plan C,' okay? Now, it's..." He sighed and rubbed the nape of his neck while smiling wearily. He said, "It's unconventional. Maybe a better word for it would be 'taboo.' So, let me try to soften the blow before I tell you my real idea, alright? So, let's say I told you to... fuck her."

"*What?*"

"Exactly," Kasper said as he pointed at him. "That's the response I wanted. You think that's crazy, right?"

Max said, "No shit. It's insane, man. What good would fu... fu..." '*Fucking.*' He couldn't say that word while talking about a corpse. He asked, "What good would doing 'that' do for us?"

"Listen, listen. I wasn't being serious. I was just telling you to *pretend* like that's my idea so you wouldn't overreact when I told you my *real* Plan C. So, now that that's out of your system, I need you to stay calm and just listen to what I'm saying. You need to seriously consider this, okay?"

"Yeah, okay. As long as it doesn't involve sex or any sick shit like that... I'm listening."

They sat in silence for a minute while Kasper carefully planned his explanation. Max was eager to hear his idea and end the night.

Kasper said, "The toilet. While you were out, I was thinking about the toilet. The bigger pieces aren't going to go down. We both know that now. So, we're left with two options. The first one: You chop her up into little pieces and try to transport her out of here in your luggage. You might need some garbage bags, too. You already assessed the risks of that plan. People might notice the blood. You could walk out of here with her head in a bag and that bag could rip open in the lobby. Then what do you have? You have a severed head bouncing on the floor like a soccer ball in front of everyone. It's very risky, right?"

Max stayed quiet.

Kasper said, "So your second option—my Plan C—is: Eat her."

"Wha–What?"

"Don't yell, okay? I know it's absurd already. Hell, it's batshit insane. We're talking straitjackets-at-a-maximum-security-mental-hospital crazy. But hear me out.

You were perfectly fine flushing her down the toilet, right? So, eat her, digest her, then shit her out and flush her later."

"What the fuck, man?" Max responded with a quivering voice.

Kasper scrunched up half his face and waved his hand. He said, "That came out wrong. I thought it would lighten the mood, but it was just morbid. But my point stands. If you eat her, you can—in a sense—hide her *in* your body and then flush her into the sewage system. No one would be able to find her then. Maybe it's morbid for me to say this, too, but... it's the perfect crime. You don't even have to eat all of her. Just the big pieces that won't flush or fit in your luggage."

Plan C, Max thought. *And 'C' is for Cannibalism.* He felt queasy just thinking about eating another human. It wasn't natural. It was beyond morbid. It was wicked —*ungodly.*

Fingers buried in his hair and knees up to his face, he said, "I don't think I can do something like that. I mean, even if I thought I could, I wouldn't know where to start. I'm not an animal, Kasper, I can't just go in there and tear her apart with my damn teeth."

"Listen to me, Max. If you want to get out of this, you better start thinking like an animal. If you're worried about what people are going to think about you, stop it. Stop considering any of that crap. You already took her life and tried flushing her down the toilet. You're already headline news, bud."

"But we're talking about eating someone. I mean,

it's easy for you to say it, but *I* have to go through with it. There's a big difference."

Kasper shrugged and asked, "Then what do you want to do? You want to chop her up into little pieces and roll her out of here in your suitcase? Where are you going to take her? Hmm? You're just going to keep her rotting flesh in your trunk and hope no one notices? At the end of the day, it's easier to bury bones than to bury flesh. So, what's it going to be?"

Max considered some potential dumping grounds. *His home?* Andrea would notice the stench within minutes. *The woods?* Everyone searched the woods when someone went missing. *His car's trunk?* He was unstable. He couldn't trust himself to drive straight, so he was expecting to be pulled over as soon as he left the hotel. He thought about asking Kasper to allow him to hide the corpse in his home, but he already knew the answer.

NO.

Chaos ran rampant in his mind. There were no angels on his shoulders, only devils whispering terrible ideas into his ears. Cannibalism seemed like the best option.

Max asked, "If I went through with it, where would I start? You have any ideas?"

Kasper stood from the bed and said, "You start by getting dressed and washing up."

"I didn't really agree to anything yet. I was just–"

"You know you're going to do it, Maxie, so stop wasting our time."

Max detected the stoniness in Kasper's voice. He did as he was told in order to avoid knocking down his only pillar of support. He went into the bathroom, eyes up to avoid the corpse in the luggage. He washed the blood off himself at the sink and got dressed.

From the doorway, Kasper said, "You're going to go to the department store next door. It's kinda like a mall, but it's open 24/7. They got a floor with a grocery store, a pharmacy, a floor with electronics... You're going to go there and you're going to buy an electric grill. You're also going to buy some garlic, onions, salt, and pepper. You're going to use it to season the 'meat.' I'm hoping the garlic and onions will mask the smell, too. Maybe you should buy a plunger while you're out there. Just in case, you know?"

As he buttoned his shirt, Max said, "It sounds like you thought this through already."

"Because I did. I'm only looking out for you, my man."

"But... it's just shopping. I know I can't ask you for much, but couldn't you just do this for me?"

"No," Kasper said. "It would make me an accomplice. Now, if you get caught—and I said '*if*,' so don't freak out, okay?—I can say I stuck around here because I was scared or I was restrained. Something like that, you know? If I go out there and start buying things for you to use on her, they're going to have a case against me. They'll say: 'Why did you buy that for him? Why didn't you run when you left the room?

Why did you go back? Why didn't you call the cops?' I can't fuck myself over like that. I'm sorry."

Max understood him. Kasper was always two steps ahead when it came to his safety. He was a kind man, but he wasn't going to go to prison for someone else.

"I get it," Max said. He turned to face him and asked, "How do I look? Am I clean?"

"Give me a spin, champ."

Max spun around with his arms up. His hands were stained pink by Katie's blood. A few drops of blood had landed on his shirt, too.

Kasper asked, "You have a jacket?"

"In the closet."

"Good. Put it on, don't take it off for anything or anyone, and you'll be fine."

"You sure?"

"I'm positive, Max."

Max grabbed the suit jacket from the closet and put it on. It covered the dried blood spattered on the chest and sleeves of his shirt. He spun around in front of Kasper again.

Kasper said, "You're good to go. Just remember to stay calm. No one knows what happened here. Understand? There's no reason for you to panic out there. Okay?"

"Okay."

"I'll be here when you get back."

Max looked out at the vacant hallway through the peephole. He breathed deeply, then he cracked the door open and slunk out of the room. He hurried down the corridor. To his utter surprise, it didn't stretch or tilt. He didn't hear or see any other guests, either. He called the elevator, then he went down to the first floor.

He observed a man sitting in the lobby, a cell phone in his hand and a suitcase next to his seat. Two women stood behind the check-in counter, chatting about their night. The concierge desk was closed. He felt like everyone was watching him, so he smiled and waved at them. But no one noticed him. And even if they did, no one cared. He was just another guest at a hotel.

He exited through the front doors and headed to the department store.

8

COOKS

The lock *beeped*.

Max turned the handle and pushed the door open, two plastic bags rustling in his hands. He kicked the door shut behind him, then he fastened the swing bar lock with his nose.

"Kasper," Max said as he looked through the peephole. "I did it. Holy shit, I actually did it. I got the stuff. And... And no one noticed anything. No one followed me. No one even said a thing to me. It was just a regular trip to the store. Just like you said, man."

A smile of relief and pride blossomed on Max's face. Then his smile flipped into a frown of puzzlement. Kasper didn't answer him. He stepped into the bathroom doorway. Every few seconds, a drop of blood dripped from Katie's knuckles. The light continued humming, too. He stepped into the bedroom and placed the bags on the entertainment center.

"Kasper?" Max said. "Kasper?! What the hell is

this? What are you trying to pull? Huh? Where are you?!"

There was no response. Max ran through the hotel room. Like a kid playing hide-and-seek, he searched all of the obvious hiding places. *Behind the window curtains?* No one. *Under the bed?* No one. *In the bathtub?* No one. He even checked the sink cabinet, as if an adult male could fit in there, but it was empty. He looked at the closet.

He shouted, "What the hell, Kasper?!" He opened the closet door—but there was no one in there. He stuttered, "Wha–What the fuck? Whe–Where... Kasper, where'd you go?"

He took two steps back, eyebrows knitted in horrified awe. He felt his throat tightening, his heartbeat accelerating, and his legs swaying. His life came crashing down. He had pushed himself so hard, sacrificed so much, just to be abandoned by his closest friend. He could take a life, but he couldn't get away with murder by himself. *It's over,* he thought.

"No, no, no, no, no," he muttered quickly.

"Max, what are you doing over there?"

Max shut his eyes so tightly that they started to sting. He recognized the voice—*John Kasper*. But he had searched every nook and cranny in the room. No one else was in there.

Was there?

He turned slowly to face the bedroom, then he opened his eyes. He staggered upon spotting Kasper sitting on one of the wingback chairs, his legs crossed and fingers interlocked over his crotch.

Kasper asked, "So, how did the shopping go?" Max was speechless. Kasper pouted and asked, "You alright, buddy?"

"How did you do that?" Max asked.

"Do what?"

"You... You weren't here. You disappeared, then you... you appeared all of a sudden. It's impossible, but I know what I saw. I checked everywhere and you weren't here... and now you're here. What the hell is going on?"

"Umm... Well, shit, Maxie, I don't know what you're talking about. I've been sitting here this whole time. You walked in here, you put the bags next to the TV, then you went to the closet and hung up your jacket."

"I did not hang up my..."

Max looked down at himself. His jacket was gone. He looked into the closet and saw it hanging from the rod.

"What the hell?" he whispered. "I didn't... No, this is impossible. I didn't take it off. And you weren't sitting there. I'm not crazy. I am *not* crazy, okay?"

Kasper said, "No one said you were crazy, bud. I'm just trying to help you stay grounded, you know?"

"No, you're fucking with me," Max said as he marched up to him. "That's what you're doing, isn't it? You're trying to fuck with my head so you can... so you can trick me, right? You're trying to pull a fast one on me. You always do this. You did it before. You're here one second and you're gone the next. And I'm sick of it."

Kasper leaned back in his seat and put his hands on the armrests. He said, "Max, I'm telling you the truth. I've been sitting here for fifteen, maybe twenty minutes. In plain sight, okay? I saw you walk in, drop the bags, then take off your coat. That's how *I* saw it."

"That's a lie!"

"It's not! Listen, buddy, you're losing control of yourself again. I'm not saying you're going crazy, but the stress is obviously getting to you. I have no doubt about that. You have to calm down if you want to get through this. Seriously, have you even been listening to yourself? Who do you think I am? Houdini?"

"It's just... I saw... You weren't here. I know what I saw."

"It was the stress—the stress and the adrenaline. I'm here, aren't I? You didn't see me on the phone, did you? You didn't hear me talking to anyone, either, right? Just relax. Forget about this for a minute. Let's push past it. Did you get everything?"

Max stepped back until his legs hit the mattress, then he sat at the foot of the bed. The rules of nature didn't apply to that floor of the hotel. He sought a rational explanation, but his mind hit one dead end after another. Nothing made sense to him. He clenched his fists and drove his fingernails into his palms, hoping the pain would wake him from a nightmare.

But he was already awake.

He said, "I, uh... I got the stuff. The electric grill, a plunger, some garlic and onion, salt and pepper, barbecue sauce..."

"Oh, that's perfect," Kasper said. "To get it down easier, right? Nice thinking."

"Tha–Thanks."

"What else?"

"Uh... Some knives. I bought a set of knives to make it a little easier to... to cut her up. It even came with a cleaver."

"*Nice*. Great job."

Max was disgusted by Kasper's gleeful, congratulatory tone. He killed Katie, but he felt like he was cleaning up Kasper's mess.

Kasper said, "Now take off your clothes. It's going to be a lot bloodier this time, so I recommend getting naked. If not, at least strip down to your underwear."

Head down, eyes glazed, Max stood from the bed and disrobed himself. After losing track of his jacket earlier, he was surprised he wasn't already undressed. His underwear stayed on. He stacked his folded clothes on the nightstand.

Kasper asked, "Now, are you sure you don't want to take your boxers off? Better safe than sorry, don't you think?"

"I don't want to be naked in front of you," Max said as he sat across from him.

"It's not like I haven't seen it before," Kasper responded with a smirk.

"Huh? Wait a second. You–You've never seen me naked before."

They gazed into each other's eyes for thirty chillingly quiet seconds. There was joy in Kasper's and confusion in Max's.

"Forget about it," Kasper said. "You have a game plan?"

"Not really."

"Okay, so let me start by telling you what I know and what I think I know. First, avoid the brain and the small intestines. If you eat those, you may get... I think they call 'em prion diseases. Those are brain-eating diseases. If I remember correctly, they're always fatal —*always*. I think you should play it safe and start with her muscles."

Max choked down the lump in his throat, then he asked, "What about the blood?"

"What about it?"

"Don't they, like, uh... In slaughterhouses, don't they bleed the animals out?"

Kasper shrugged and said, "I guess so. You could do that, but it depends on the clock. How much time do you have left? How many nights did you book?"

Max said, "Just one."

Kasper checked his Rolex and said, "It's already past midnight. You have to check out at eleven. That's in less than ten hours. You think you have enough time to hang her and bleed her, then clean this mess up? 'Cause I don't."

The clock was ticking. Max kicked himself for

wasting too much time crying and arguing. Although he questioned everything, he had gone too far to turn back. He was determined to end his living nightmare.

He said, "Then let's just get it over with."

Kasper stood in the bathroom doorway, arms crossed. Max squatted beside the suitcase with a chef's knife in hand. The electric grill—large enough to cook six hamburgers at a time—sat near the sink, plugged into an outlet next to the mirror. Chopped onion and garlic cooked on it, helping mask the corpse's stench. His condiments stood beside the grill. Five more knives were laid out in the bathtub: A cleaver, a santoku knife, a boning knife, a paring knife, and a steak knife.

Max asked, "You sure I won't get sick if I, uh… if I 'consume' her muscles?"

'Consume.' That word didn't roll off Max's tongue, it sounded awkward and unnatural, but he couldn't say *'eat,'* either. He agreed to commit an act of cannibalism, but it didn't mean he was proud of it.

Kasper said, "I'm positive. Just do it exactly like I told you."

Max rolled her onto her stomach without taking her out of the suitcase. He tucked her mangled hands under her stomach so he wouldn't have to see them. Rigor mortis started stiffening her limbs. He rubbed the back of her leg. Her skin was cooling down, but she wasn't cold to the core yet. He slid the blade across her hindquarters.

On her left leg, he pressed the blade under her ass cheek with enough pressure to cut her horizontally. One drop of blood ran down to her genitals and another drop crawled down her outer thigh. With the blade in the gash, he angled the knife and slid it down her leg, skinning her thigh. He could hear her skin shredding under the hum of the light. He severed the flap of skin above her popliteal fossa—her 'kneepit.'

He was sickened by her exposed muscle—pink but bloody, hard but stringy. He closed his eyes and bit his bottom lip. Like a man struggling with premature ejaculation, he started solving simple math problems in his head to distract himself. *One plus one equals two, two plus two equals four, four plus four equals eight, eight plus eight equals sixteen.*

"Keep going," Kasper said. "You're doing good, Maxie. Real good."

Sixteen plus sixteen equals thirty-two.

Max released a long, controlled exhale. Under her ass cheek, he sliced her leg again. He flayed the skin next to her exposed muscle. Splashes of blood jumped out at him, causing him to flinch. He severed the skin above her kneepit and watched it slide between her thighs. He noticed some dark blue veins around her muscles.

He set the knife down beside him, then he grabbed the santoku knife from the bathtub. It functioned like a chef's knife, but it was lighter, allowing for smoother, more precise cuts. He stabbed her exposed hamstring just below her ass. He angled the knife to bury it under the muscle, then he sawed into it. He cut a circular piece of muscle off her—a round steak. He could see her bone in the crater.

He struggled to his feet with the flesh in one hand and the knife in the other. He hesitated for a moment. The look on his face said: *Am I really going to go through with this?*

Kasper said, "You've got this, man."

Max threw the human steak on the electric grill. The blood immediately sizzled, feathers of smoke rising from the steak. He salted and peppered it, then swiped some of the burned onion and garlic at it with the knife. A strong beefy, metallic aroma attacked his nostrils and stung his eyes. He couldn't stand there and watch it cook.

He crouched beside the suitcase and sawed into the center of her hamstring. The tears in his eyes made it easier for him. Everything looked red. He couldn't fear what he couldn't see. He cut an egg-shaped steak off her leg. He tossed it on the grill, then he flipped the other chunk of muscle. The first piece was brown already. He sprinkled some more salt and pepper on the human flesh.

Stay busy, he told himself.

He went down and started cutting into her hamstring again. He tried to sever a piece of her muscle near her kneepit, but there wasn't very much of it down there. The tip of the blade kept scraping her femur and sliding out of her. He turned his attention to her ass—soft but firm. It seemed like the perfect source of protein.

He cut into the small of her back horizontally, angled the knife, then dragged it down, following the voluptuous curve of her ass. The blade glided under her skin while cutting into her gluteus medius and gluteus maximus.

"Attaboy," Kasper whispered under his breath, smiling deviously.

Max stopped before he could sever the skin. He caught a glimpse of the feces smeared around her anus. He sniffled, then he hiccupped. He felt vomit brewing in his gut. Kasper could see him breaking down. He couldn't allow him to scream so close to the front door. He had to distract him to save themselves.

He said, "Hey, it's done. I think it's burning. Maxie, hey, don't let it burn or they'll smell it."

Max grabbed the edge of the sink and pulled himself up to his feet. Using the knife as a spatula, he lifted the larger steak off the grill and placed it on the counter, then he flipped the other piece and peppered it again. He stared at the well-done human steak—grayish-brown, a bit charred. The color was drained from his face. He was afraid—*so very afraid*.

Kasper said, "Remember, it's just food. Don't think of it as anything else but food."

"*Mm–hmm,*" Max hummed in agreement, unable to say a word.

He popped the bottle of barbecue sauce open and

slathered it on the meat. He pulled his lips into his mouth and licked them, but he couldn't moisten them. The meal was unappealing. No matter how hard he tried, he couldn't convince himself that *humans* were *food*. In civilized societies, people didn't eat other people.

Kasper said, "There are other options, but you'll never know if this would have worked if you don't give it your all. Eat it. *Now*."

Max snorted his mucus up before it could spill out of his nose. He wiped his eyes, then he stabbed the steak with his knife. He raised it up to his face and looked at himself in the mirror. His hands and forearms were covered in blood. Some drops landed on his neck, chest, and underwear. *What have I become?*—he thought.

He closed his eyes and bit into the meat. He gagged as a squirt of blood shot out and hit the back of his throat. The meat was tough. He sank his teeth into it again and shook his head until he tore a piece off. The barbecue sauce helped hide the taste of human flesh, but he could still taste the tang of blood. He chewed on it for thirty seconds. It wasn't getting easier.

So, he turned on the faucet, filled a cup with water, then threw his head back and guzzled it down. He felt the meat moving down his esophagus, as if he had swallowed a tennis ball.

"Fuck me," he whined.

"You got this," Kasper cheered. "The hard part is over. You can finish this, my man!"

"Fu–Fuck me," Max repeated in a quavering voice.

He poured more barbecue sauce on the other half of the steak, then he bit it off the knife. His right cheek inflated as he chewed on it. He felt like he was gnawing on an entire pack of Big League Chew bubble gum. Despite his grinding and chomping, his teeth couldn't tear through it. The taste of her blood made his tongue and gums tingle.

He flooded his mouth with barbecue sauce, drinking it straight from the bottle. Tears went down his cheeks as he swallowed the flesh. He gasped for air while rubbing his neck. He felt a lump in his throat, sending him into near-hysteria. *I'm choking, I'm choking, I'm choking,* he thought. He chugged one cup of water after another, big streams of the liquid running down his chin.

Kasper clapped and said, "Well done, my friend, well done." He pointed at the grill and said, "Hey, that one's getting a little crispy. You should eat it before it burns."

Max stabbed the meat with the knife and took it off the grill. The steak landed on the counter next to the sink. He looked at his reflection while catching his breath. Traces of blood gave color to his pale lips. He wiped his mouth with his palms, unintentionally smearing more blood on his face.

"Goddammit," he muttered.

Kasper asked, "What are you waiting for?"

"I can't do it."

"Are you kidding me? You already did it. There's no point in–"

"I mean, I can't do it *now*, Kasper. It's... I'm... I feel a little sick, alright? I just need to make sure I can keep it down. I'll keep cutting and cooking, but I can't eat 'it' right now. Okay?"

"Yeah, yeah. I guess that makes sense. You don't want to throw up and make a bigger mess, right? But just remember, Maxie, you don't have all night."

Max knelt beside the suitcase. He shoved a wad of toilet paper in Katie's ass to block his view of her feces, then he thrust the blade at her exposed gluteus maximus. He carved a circle into the muscle, listening to the fibers tear and vessels burst. Her gluteal muscles were stronger than her hamstrings, so Max had a hard time sawing through it.

Drops of blood raced across her ass. It filled her butt crack, like rain flooding a canal, and soaked the toilet paper.

Then a geyser of blood flew out of her ass as he severed her superior gluteal artery. It entered his mouth and splashed in his eyes. He leaned back and dodged the second squirt of blood. The knife protruded from her ass, sticking out of her thick muscle.

"Ah shit," he whimpered.

The blood kept spurting out in a circular motion, like water from a rotary sprinkler. The bleeding slowed after ten seconds, but it didn't completely stop.

Kasper said, "Don't panic. You have this under

control. Just cut it out and it'll stop. Come on, man, you can do this."

Max reluctantly crawled back to the suitcase. He pressed his fingers against her exposed muscle and wiggled the knife with his other hand. He saw blood bubbling out from the curved laceration. As soon as the knife reached the initial incision, he pinched the muscle and tugged on it. Then another squirt of blood flew out and hit his face.

The chunk of muscle came off and he fell back against the cupboard. He spat her blood out of his mouth. He dry-heaved and shuddered upon spotting the hole of mushy flesh on her ass.

Kasper said, "Toss it on the grill and get yourself something to drink. Seriously, you don't look too good."

Max rose to his feet, his legs shaking. He placed Katie's ass on the grill. The *sizzle* of her blood made his ears ring. It was unusually loud.

He plugged his ears with his bloody index fingers and yelled, "God, stop it!"

"Max!" Kasper shouted. "Max, relax! Drink some water!"

"I can still hear it!"

"Max!"

Max staggered back. He slid on Katie's blood, then he lost his footing on the suitcase. He fell back and landed between the bathtub and the toilet. The back of his head hit the wall, knocking him unconscious. It all went black, but he could still hear her blood sizzling.

9

NIGHTMARES OF… MEMORIES?

"Are you homeless?" Max asked, crouching in front of a skinny, filthy man in tattered clothes.

Jay Jones stared back at him, sitting beside a dumpster with his back against a brick wall. The bemused look on his face said: *No shit*. They were in an alley between two tall apartment buildings. Every few minutes, a pedestrian walked down the sidewalk just a couple of meters away.

"What gave it away?" Jay asked sarcastically. "My beard? My clothes? *My stink?*"

Max smiled and said, "I've met people with longer beards, dirtier clothes, and worse smells at my workplace." He pointed at his legs and said, "It was your feet."

"What about 'em?"

"You're not wearing any shoes."

"Oh, is that right? Well, guess I must have forgot 'em at home."

"So, you're not homeless?"

Jay furrowed his brow and tilted his head back. The answer was obvious, but Max seemed oblivious. He looked him over. Max was dressed in a suit, holding a plastic bag with a large glass bottle inside. His briefcase stood on the ground next to him. He looked like he had just gotten off work.

Max chuckled, then he said, "I'm kidding." Jay responded with an insincere laugh, then he rolled his eyes and looked away. Max pointed at the tin can beside Jay and asked, "Is that yours?"

"Yeah, as a matter of fact, it is," Jay said. He shook it at Max, coins jingling inside. He said, "And from now on, you're goin' to have to give me a little 'contribution' for every dumb question you ask me. And if you ain't got no contributions for me, I ain't got no time for you. Got it?"

"Loud and clear."

Max pulled his wallet out of his pocket. He took a five-dollar bill out and tossed it into Jay's can. Jay looked at the can, then he squinted at Max. He was just trying to give him a hard time, so he wasn't actually expecting him to pay him.

"What do you want from me?" Jay asked.

Still smiling, Max responded, "Now does your rule work the other way around? You know, every time you ask *me* a dumb question, you have to give *me* a little contribution?"

"What do you want from me?" Jay repeated as he lowered the tin can.

"I'm sorry. I was just trying to lighten the mood. Listen, I'm interested in your story. I'll give you some money for every 'dumb' question I ask. And I'll walk away right now if you don't want that. Okay?"

Jay didn't feel threatened by Max. The young man looked meek and awkward. But the situation was bizarre. Men in suits didn't often stop to talk to homeless people in alleys, especially at the dead of night. He knew Max had ulterior motives. At the same time, it was hard to say 'no' to easy money. He shook the can at him.

Max threw another five-dollar bill inside and asked, "How long have you been homeless?"

"Four years and three months."

Another five-dollar bill landed in Jay's can.

Max asked, "You have any family in the area? Mama? Papa? A wife? Kids?"

"I got an ex-wife and a baby girl. Well, she ain't a baby no more. She's fourteen or... fifteen now. I don't know, maybe sixteen. Haven't seen my family in three years."

"Why'd you split up? Why haven't you seen them in so long?"

Jay wagged the tin can at him. Max threw a five-dollar bill inside.

Jay shook the can again and said, "You asked two dumb questions that time."

Max snickered, then he said, "You're right, you're right." He took a twenty dollar bill out of his wallet and showed it to the homeless man. As he put it in the can, he said, "This should be enough to cover a few questions, right?"

Jay said, "We'll see."

"So, why'd you split from them? Why haven't you seen your family recently?"

"You want the truth?" Jay asked, sneering.

Max nodded.

Jay said, "Alright, sure. I'll tell ya the story. You see, I was stupid with our money. Bad investments, dumb gambles, and 'avoidable' scams. That's what my wife called 'em. 'Avoidable.' She forgave me, sure, then I started drinking more and more. And when I get drunk, I get mean. So, I hit her. More than once. More than I can remember as a matter of fact. I couldn't get a job, I couldn't get my act together, so we lost the house and she ran off to live with her mother. I tried fixing things, but... they wouldn't take me back. I get it, too. They got their lives together, I didn't." He interlocked his fingers repeatedly and said, "We just couldn't reconnect. You know how it is, don't ya?"

Max was no longer smiling. He asked, "So, they don't know if you're dead or alive out here, do they? You don't have a connection to anyone? I mean, do you even have any friends out here?"

"I'm not out here 'cause I'm looking for 'connections.' I'm out here 'cause I ain't got no other choice."

"So, do you have friends or not?"

"What kind of question is that? Why are you even asking me any of this shit? Huh? What's wrong with you, boy?"

Max didn't respond. A yellow taxi rolled down the neighboring street and a woman walked her French Bulldog past the alley.

Max coughed to clear his throat, then he said, "Hypothetically speaking, if you were to go missing, no one would ever miss you, right?"

Jay glared at him, as if he could push him away with his eyes. He said, "Sure. Guess you're right."

"You're exactly the type of person I've been looking for: *A nobody*. Nobody misses nobodies, eh?"

"What the fuck are you talking about, man?"

"It doesn't really matter."

"You're one strange motherfu–"

Max slapped the tin can out of Jay's hand. Dollar bills, crumpled and folded, flew out and landed on the garbage bags next to him while coins of all sizes bounced and rolled on the ground.

"What the hell's your problem, man?!" Jay barked.

He kept muttering about Max as he scrambled to pick up the money. He threw himself onto the garbage bags and grabbed the bills first. The twenty-dollar bill landed in a puddle of brown liquid on one of the bags. He straightened it out, waved it a few times, then folded it and returned it to his can. Then he picked up the coins. He couldn't afford to lose even a penny.

When it came to homelessness, every cent mattered.

Meanwhile, Max took a heavy bottle of red wine out of the plastic bag. He held it from its neck as he walked slowly behind the homeless man, like a predator stalking his prey. Jay stopped upon spotting Max's shadowy reflection on a puddle.

He mumbled, "Wha–What are you–"

Before he could turn around, Max swung the bottle down at Jay and struck the back of his head. The bottle broke, the sound of glass shattering echoing through the narrow alleyway. Jay fell to the ground face first, blood spewing out from the gash at the top of his head. His scalp was split open. Wine and blood soaked his hair, red drops dripping from the frizzy, matted locks. The blood trickled out from his hair, flowing down his cheeks and forehead. Some of it reached his thick beard.

Jay pushed himself up to his hands and knees, but he couldn't stop his arms from wobbling. He quickly collapsed again.

"Look at what you made me do," Max said. "I just got a promotion, man. I was going to drink this and celebrate with my fiancé. But you wouldn't know anything about that, huh? You miserable bastard."

He bent over and dusted the bloody glass shards out of Jay's hair with his hand. Just as Jay crawled forward an inch, Max swung the broken bottle at the back of his head. His face crashed into the floor, breaking his nose and cracking his frontal bone. Another gash stretched from the curve at the back of his head to the nape of his neck. The large cuts were surrounded by a dozen smaller lacerations. Some shards of glass were buried *in* his scalp.

Max only held the neck of the bottle now. He shook

his head in disappointment as he tossed it at the garbage bags.

As he reached into the plastic bag, he said, "You owe me some... 'red wine.' Don't worry, I know just how to get it."

He pulled a corkscrew out of the bag, then he crumpled the bag up and tossed it at the garbage. A pickup truck cruised past the alleyway, followed by a sedan, and then another taxi. More lights went out than turned on above them. Some of the neighbors had heard the shattering glass, but no one bothered to check on the noise. It was normal in that area.

Max stepped on the back of Jay's head and, with a jolly grin, he asked, "You still awake?"

Jay groaned as the pavement scraped his face. Shards of glass stabbed his forehead and cheeks. He inhaled deeply, unwittingly pulling slivers of glass into his eyes and breathing some in. One of his eyes turned bloodshot. A bloody tear seeped out, dripping down his cheek like red mascara on a crying teenager's face.

He said, "Get... Get..." He coughed as the glass irritated his throat. He grabbed Max's ankle and said, "Get... off me."

Dazed by the blows to the head and weak from years of malnourishment, Jay couldn't overpower him. So, he slid his hand under the hem of Max's pants and clawed at his ankle.

"*Ow!*" Max yelped as he took his foot off Jay's head. "Oh, you're going to pay for that, you dirty bastard."

Jay tried to stand, but Max knelt on his back and

pinned him to the ground. He grabbed Jay's limp arm and lifted his hand up to his chest. He hooked the corkscrew's bottle opener under his long, yellow fingernail, then he flicked it up. Jay bellowed through his clenched teeth as his fingernail snapped off.

"Hurts, doesn't it?!" Max yelled.

"Fuck!" Jay shouted. "Fuck you!"

Max slid forward and put his knee on the back of Jay's neck with just enough pressure to smother his voice. Jay wheezed, unable to draw a satisfying breath. He flailed his limbs under Max, his feet splashing in the puddles.

Max shouted, "You should have played nice! We could have made this easy!"

Jay gagged as Max buried his knee deeper into his neck. He heard his cervical spine *popping*. Max hooked the bottle opener under Jay's middle fingernail, then flicked it up. The fingernail broke in half and cut his cuticle. A layer of blood covered the gummy flesh under his fingernail. He moved to his ring finger and snapped the fingernail off. It landed in front of Jay's face.

Max tried to remove his pinky nail, but he couldn't get a grip on it. Instead, he put his pinky through the bottle opener's ring, then jerked it upward. A long, pained groan burst out of Jay's gaping mouth as his finger broke in half. It was turned upward at a perfect 90-degree angle. An electrifying pain shot through his arm. His heart pounded so fast that he felt it bouncing off the pavement.

"S–Stop," he croaked out. "I–I can–can't... breathe."

"So, you can't breathe, huh?" Max said. "You can talk, but you can't breathe? Guess that makes sense... somehow. I should give you a hand, shouldn't I? Yeah, let me do that. Let me help you out."

Max drew the corkscrew's serrated foil cutter—a short one-inch blade. He thrust it at the side of Jay's neck, swinging it at him with all of the strength he could muster. It was too short to cut his esophagus or trachea from that angle, but it was sharp enough to easily tear through his muscles. He even trimmed some of his bloodied beard hairs.

Jay didn't realize he was being cut until the fifth stab. It felt like he was being pinched at first—hot, *stinging* pinches.

He groaned again, weaker this time, and slapped his bloody hand over his neck. Max started stabbing the back of his hand. The blade wasn't long enough to skewer his hand and pierce his neck at the same time, though. So, he thrust it at his face. The blade sliced his jaw, poked holes in his cheek, nicked his cheekbone, and then plunged into his right eye.

Jay tried to yell for help, but he could only grunt and groan and *gurgle*. The right side of his vision blurred, then it reddened, and then it blackened. Max wiggled the blade inside of his eye, like a key in a rusty lock. A string of slimy blood hung out and dangled over his nose. Jay grabbed Max's wrist with his stabbed hand.

Max seized the opportunity. He took the blade out

of his eye, then he thrust it back at his neck. He sawed into his throat until he severed his jugular. Blood sprayed out in a thick arc, visible even in the darkness of the night. Jay knew something was wrong. The burning pain was normal now, but the sudden lethargy was alarming. He felt like the life was being drained out of him through his neck—*because it was.*

He covered the wound with his hand, but it wasn't enough to stop the bleeding. The blood oozed out from under his palm and puddled under his head. His vision blurred in his left eye. Max felt his convulsions weakening. He still twitched and snorted, though. The homeless man was alive but dying.

"That's a lot of 'wine,' isn't it?" Max asked as he examined the blood. "But don't die just yet. I'm not finished with you."

He pushed the tip of the corkscrew's worm into Jay's right ear. He turned it like a valve, driving it into his ear canal. Jay felt the tension in his ear as the canal widened. He closed his eyes tightly and groaned. Then the worm ruptured his eardrum. A loud buzzing sound attacked his head. Thick, mucus-like blood dripped out of his ear.

He opened his eyes and mouth as wide as humanly possible. It looked like he was screaming, but nothing came out of his mouth. He saw the ground tilting under him.

Max kept turning the corkscrew, drilling it deeper into his head. It mutilated his inner ear, sending more goops of blood out, then it broke through his skull and cut into his brain. Jay's eyes narrowed. His lips moved as if he were saying something, but he was still quiet. Despite the resistance, Max turned the corkscrew again. He heard his brain *squelch* in his skull.

Jay stopped moving—not a breath or a twitch. Max sighed, then he glanced around. He saw another taxi cruise past the alley. A few lights were on upstairs. He could even hear an episode of HBO's *Game of Thrones* playing from an open window on the third floor of the building to his left. He didn't hear any emergency sirens, though.

No one noticed the violent murder—the public execution—of Jay Jones.

Max smiled as he stood up. He wiped his bloody hands on Jay's coat, then he adjusted his jacket and walked over to his briefcase. He took a water bottle out of his bag and used the water to wash his hands. Then he exited the alley and headed to the closest liquor store to buy another bottle of red wine for his celebration with his fiancé.

10

REASONS

MAX JERKED AND GASPED AS HE AWOKE. HE FOUND himself sitting on the floor between the toilet and the bathtub, his bare feet next to the suitcase's handle. He caught a whiff of the awful stench of charred flesh, but the sizzling had stopped. The electric grill's automatic shut-off function activated once it had reached a certain temperature.

He grabbed the edge of the bathtub and the rim of the toilet bowl to help him up. He grunted as a throbbing pain emanated from the back of his head.

"You took quite the blow," Kasper said. Max looked to his left and saw him sitting in the doorway. Kasper met his frightened gaze and, smirking, he asked, "Was that another one of those... 'nightmares of a dream?' Couldn't really tell. You laughed, you gasped, you cried. What happened this time, bud?"

Max remembered *every* grisly detail of his dream—from the moment it started to the moment it ended. As far as he knew, dreams didn't have beginnings. They always started in the middle—during the second act. But it was as if a movie had been playing in his head while he was unconscious.

He sat on the edge of the bathtub and stared vacantly at Katie's defiled corpse. He said, "I think something's wrong with me."

"Yeah," Kasper said. "I'm pretty sure we already knew that."

"No, I mean something's *seriously* wrong with me."

"Okay, I'm listening. It's usually not a good idea to self-diagnose, but what do *you* think is wrong with *you*, Maxie?"

Max looked down at his clasped hands and said, "I... I have violent thoughts."

Kasper responded, "I know that already. I think that's kinda normal. Everyone wants to beat up the slow driver or the obnoxious caller."

Max said, "You know that's not what I mean. These thoughts... They get in my head and they stay there. They tell me... No, they *command* me to hurt people—to kill them. And I can't push them out. It's impossible. I've tried everything. Video games, movies, work, masturbation. Those thoughts, those voices, just keep stabbing my brain. It's like, uh..." He chuckled nervously, then he said, "I guess it's like OCD for psychopaths."

He snickered again, but there was no joy in his laughter. He didn't think it was funny, either. He just didn't know how to react to his own confession.

"I get you," Kasper said.

Max shook his head and said, "No you don't. No one understands me because I don't even understand myself. S–So, how could anyone say they know me better than me? People like you... you say you 'get me' because you're scared of me. You want to 'appease' me, right? You want to make sure I don't snap, huh?"

"That's not it. So, maybe I don't get you. Maybe I used the wrong words at the wrong time. But I think you get yourself. You just need to hear your thoughts, your reasons, out loud. So, tell me, Max—tell yourself —when did these thoughts start? What else have they been telling you?"

Max's gaze was pulled towards Katie's corpse. He thought about Andrea and his unborn child as well as the homeless man in the alley.

He said, "A few months ago, I started thinking about... about killing Andrea. She didn't do anything to deserve it. It wasn't like she attacked me or she cheated on me or she was going to leave me. We were doing fine. Then this voice... Something kept telling me to 'do it.' One night, when we were making love, I grabbed her throat and I–I choked her a little. She didn't mind at first, but then that thought got bigger —*louder*—and I started choking her some more. She panicked and kicked me off her. I had to act like I didn't notice anything was wrong, but I knew what I was doing."

He paused to collect himself, breathing slowly and

deeply. Stony-faced, Kasper stared at him, eyes unblinking.

Max continued, "After that, the thoughts died down for a while. When they came back, I started thinking about killing... Andrea and... and our baby. When Andrea slept, I thought about stabbing her stomach with an icepick. Right through the belly button, you know? I mean, I watched her sleep with an icepick in my hand two or three—sometimes four—nights a week. I almost did it, Kasper. I'm a fucked-up person, man."

"You're a good person with a troubled mind. You're not a lost cause. You can get away with this and you can make this right. I'm with you until the end."

"You shouldn't be."

"We've been friends for years. I know you're better than this."

Max was awed by Kasper's selflessness and bravery. Kasper risked more for Max than most people would sacrifice for their own wellbeing.

Max looked down at Katie. After blinking, he saw Andrea in the suitcase, her stomach ripped open and a fetus' legs sticking out of her mouth. His eyes widened and pupils dilated. He shut his eyes and rubbed them. Upon opening his eyes again, he saw Jay's corpse in the suitcase, a corkscrew in his ear and a steady stream of blood shooting out of his neck like tea from a teapot. He turned away, covered his mouth, and sobbed.

Kasper said, "Don't lose control."

"You have to leave," Max responded in a tight voice.

"What are you talking about, buddy?"

"I'm not well."

"I know, Max, we just–"

"No, Kasper," Max interrupted. "I'm sick. I can't tell what's real and what's not. My dreams... I'm starting to think they were memories. I think... Kasper, I think I might be a serial killer. Andrea might be dead already. I might have killed someone in an alley, too. The– There are probably others. Holy shit, I'm a serial killer, aren't I?"

Kasper stood up. Max expected him to run out of the hotel room and yell for help. A part of him wanted that. Instead, Kasper approached him.

He grabbed Max's shoulders and said, "Look at me." They locked eyes. Kasper said, "I am not leaving you behind. I've already gambled too much to let you get caught. But I suppose I can't make you do something you don't want to do. So, let's go over our options, okay? Although I wouldn't recommend it, you can turn yourself in to the police. Tell 'em what you told me and face the music. You'd have to make sure you tell 'em I was being held here against my will, though. You *have* to do that, Max. It won't help you in any legal cases, but it's only fair."

That makes sense, Max thought as he nodded.

Kasper said, "We can also do what we agreed to do: Get rid of her. I think we can make this work. We took it too far with 'Plan C' and that messed with your head. It's got you dreaming about memories that never happened."

"No, no, it was so real. It did hap–"

"That doesn't matter," Kasper said as he shook Max's shoulders. "Don't think about that right now. Dreams, nightmares, memories... Either way, it's all in the past. Think about this moment, Max."

"Wha–What do I do now?"

"You want my recommendation? You chop her up, you put her in some garbage bags, and you take her away from this hotel. Keep her in your trunk until you find somewhere to dump her. Maybe you can even find a way to get on the deep web and hire someone to help you. Just get her out of here. Then we can get to the bottom of everything else. If I'm correct, if you're just having some really bad lucid dreams, then we can get you some help. If I'm wrong... if you're right and you're a serial killer... We'll deal with that when the time comes. So, what do you think? What do you want to do?"

Max thought long and hard about it. He didn't believe he could get away with the murder of Katie Paulson. But he wanted to buy enough time to get home and check on Andrea. He didn't want to discover her fate from behind bars. And if Kasper was right about everything, if Andrea was still alive, he wanted to run away with her. He convinced himself that his intrusive thoughts were a product of his environment. *The pressure made me do it,* he reasoned. *I'm having nightmares because of my stress.*

Kasper possessed the gift of gab. He had a way with

words that made people feel safe and comfortable. Max trusted him with every fiber of his being.

He said, "You're always right, Kasper. I can't give up now. I have to see this through to the end. For Andrea, for you, for myself. But I won't... eat her anymore. I can't do that. I should have *never* tried."

"And I should have never suggested it," Kasper said, regret in his voice.

"So, I'll move her. I'll cut her up, fit her in the suitcase and some garbage bags, clean this place up, then check out and take her with me. Maybe I can find somewhere to hide her or... I don't know, maybe I can melt her with some acid or feed her to some wild animals, like in the movies or TV. What do you think? Can that work?"

"I think it's a brilliant idea."

"Thank God."

"Get yourself cleaned up. You need to go back to the department store and buy yourself some garbage bags and cleaning supplies. Don't make it *too* obvious, though. You don't want to walk through the lobby with a mop. The employees at the front desk would get suspicious. And if they do get suspicious, have some answers ready for their questions. Remember, Maxie, confidence can get you out of anything."

"Sure, sure."

Max removed his underwear. He wasn't afraid of exposing himself in front of Kasper anymore. He had already shared his deepest, darkest secrets with him. A glimpse of his dick wasn't going to change a thing. Kasper huffed and smirked. He returned to his seat at the end of the bedroom while Max cleaned and dressed himself.

"The garbage bags are going to be your primary concern," Kasper said as Max walked into the room while buttoning his shirt. "They need to be *black* and *durable*. You don't want anyone to be able to see through them and you definitely don't want them to tear."

"I understand," Max said. He sat at the foot of the bed and slid his pants up his legs, then he put on his shoes. He said, "I'll be back as soon as possible."

"I know you're scared and I know I said we're running out of time, but don't rush. A man running around a store buying cleaning supplies in the early morning will look mighty suspicious."

"I won't rush, but I'll be fast—fast and natural."

"Great. Good luck, Max."

"Thank you."

Max marched to the front door and looked through the peephole. There was no one in the hallway. He looked back at Kasper. Kasper gave him a nod, as if to say: *Go ahead, bud, you can do it*. Max returned the nod, eyes glimmering with courage. He exited the room and headed down to the lobby via the elevator.

In the lobby, he saw a man arguing with the receptionists about checking in early. It was a welcomed distraction. He headed out into the darkness of dawn's astronomical twilight.

11

SHOPPING

Max studied his reflection on a glossy flatscreen television. Although it was dark, he could see himself clearly. He finally understood what it was like to 'look like hell.' His hair stuck out in all directions. His clothing was disheveled, his bloodstained shirt hidden under his jacket. His bloodshot eyes sank into the black bags of flesh underneath them. Katie's blood turned his fingers pink, as if he were eating fistfuls of Flamin' Hot Cheetos all day.

He looked down the wall of televisions to his right. Every TV was set to a different program—cartoons, movies, news reports. Some were off and others were stuck on blue screens. There were no other customers in that section, though. He tucked his hands in his pockets and walked to the cleaning supplies area at the other end of the floor. He saw a woman pushing a cart down an aisle, browsing the bottles of window cleaners.

Did she kill someone, too?—he thought.

He stopped at the center of an aisle and examined the garbage bags. There were dozens of options: Heavy-duty, strong, extra-strong, ultra-strong, extra thick, XL, XXL, scented and unscented. He reached for the regular drawstring garbage bags he usually bought for his kitchen, but he hesitated. He never had a garbage bag rip open on him, but he never carried amputated human limbs in any garbage bags, either.

He stepped back and entered a thinking pose— one arm crossed over his abdomen and a hand stroking his chin. He thought: *Extra-strong is obviously stronger than ultra-strong. But is ultra-strong stronger than the heavy-duty bags? Does it even matter? But if I get the XXL bags, I won't have to cut her down too much. Wait a second. 'Extra'-strong? Does that mean it's extra strong compared to the 'Strong' bags or compared to the 'Ultra-Strong' bags?*

"May I help you, sir?" a male voice asked, interrupting his thoughts.

Max turned to his right and found a pudgy young man standing beside him. The name tag clinging to his red vest read: *Jared Q.* His long brown hair reached down to his shoulders. There were dark circles under his inflamed eyes. He looked like a sleepy stoner, but the same thought popped up in Max's head: *Did he kill someone, too?* Anyone and everyone could have been a killer.

"Yeah," Max said. "I'm looking for garbage bags."

Jared looked at the shelves in front of them, then

back at Max. He said, "They're right in front of you, sir."

Max chuckled, then he said, "I know, I know. I'm, uh... I'm looking for your most durable bags."

Jared said, "That would be the, um... the..." He scanned the shelves. He didn't know the answer, either, so he had to take an educated guess. He said, "The Ultra-Strong brand."

"Great. Do you have that in black?"

Jared sucked his teeth, then he said, "Doesn't look like it."

"Can you check the back?"

"Well, it doesn't look like there are any empty shelves out here, so what you see is what we've got."

"Okay, fine. What about those? Which one's more durable: Extra-Strong or Heavy-Duty?"

Jared sighed, then with a hint of uncertainty in his voice as if he were asking a question, he responded, "Heavy-duty?"

Max grabbed the box of black heavy-duty garbage bags. The garbage bags were three millimeters thick and held up to 42 gallons.

Before the sales associate could walk away, Max asked, "Can this hold a dead body?"

"*Huh?*" Jared responded, eyes beginning to widen.

Max shut his eyes and shook his head. He wanted to hit himself for asking that question. *Confidence,* he thought. He laughed and waved his hand at Jared, trying to play it cool.

He said, "Sorry, that came out wrong. I'm a little

sleepy, you know? 'A dead body,' sounds crazy now that I think of it. Anyway, I meant, like, uh... a carcass. An animal carcass. You see, I sometimes stumble upon dead animals in my neighborhood—roadkill and stuff like that—and you know this city. The government doesn't give a crap about it. They'd let the homeless shit on the streets as long as it's not in their driveway in their gated communities, right?"

"Sure," Jared said with a shrug.

"So, you think this can hold a dead animal? I wouldn't want it tearing in my car or on the sidewalk."

"I'm sure it can, sir."

"And it won't leak, right? Sometimes, these animals are still bleeding."

Jared sneered and said, "I don't need to..." He wanted to say: *I don't need to hear all of that.* But he wasn't interested in continuing their conversation. He pointed at the front of the box and said, "It says right there that it's 'leak-proof.' You're good to go, sir."

"Great, great. Thank you very much, Jared."

"Yup. Have a good one."

"I will."

Jared kept glancing back at him as he walked away. As soon as the sales associate turned the corner, Max headed in the opposite direction. He grabbed a basket at the end of the aisle and started filling it with cleaning supplies: A brush with a short handle, bleach, window cleaner, stain remover, and laundry detergent. The vinegar was in the baking aisle downstairs, so he moved it to the bottom of his list.

While looking over the products in his basket, another idea crossed his mind: *Kill two birds with one stone.* Cleaning products were filled with hazardous chemicals. Mixing certain cleaners could create deadly fumes. So, he figured there had to be a mixture that could deteriorate human flesh.

Running his eyes over the shelves, he muttered, "They have to sell some sort of acid here, right? Maybe a drain cleaner? That melts stuff, doesn't it?" From the corner of his eye, he spotted Jared patrolling the aisles. He yelled, "Jared!"

Jared had already strolled past the aisle. He considered marching forward, pretending like he didn't hear him, but he feared he'd get an earful from his manager if Max complained about him. He rolled his eyes, then he walked back to the cleaning supplies aisle. He put a slight smile on his face as he approached Max.

"Sorry, but I have another question for you," Max said.

"Shoot."

"Okay, so I told you about the dead 'animals,' right? The carcasses, remember? Let's say I wanted to *melt* those dead bodies. Can you recommend something?"

"Something to melt a carcass?" Jared asked, brow furrowed in pure befuddlement.

"Yeah, yeah. You watched Breaking Bad, right? You remember that scene where Walter and Jesse dissolve a body in a bathtub? Like in a... an acid bath, basically. Do you remember what they used? Or do you sell something like that?"

"Like... acid?"

"Yeah."

They stood in silence. Max waited for a serious answer while Jared waited for a punchline to a joke. A middle-aged woman pushed a cart towards them. Max stepped aside as she grabbed a bottle of liquid drain cleaner. She read the label like a child reading the back of a cereal box, then she tossed it in her cart and walked away.

Jared grunted, then he said, "So, uh... I don't know anything about Breaking Bad. I think I heard about that scene on a podcast a couple of years ago, but that's it. I don't *think* they used anything from the cleaning aisle, though. And I don't know anything about 'dissolving' dead animals. I thought you just threw 'em in the trash or cremated 'em."

'*Cremate.*' The word planted itself in Max's mind. He hadn't considered reducing Katie's corpse to ashes through combustion.

He said, "I thought so, too. But you know the city, you know the government. They'd rather let these carcasses rot on the streets than get rid of them properly. So, you have any suggestions?"

"Well, I can tell you we don't sell acid here. I'm not really, like, a brainiac or anything like that, either, so I have no idea about mixing these things together, but I know it's pretty dangerous if you don't know what you're doing. My boss is pretty smart, though. He used to work at a school. You want me to send him to you? I don't know if he's busy, but he's here."

'Don't make it too obvious,' Max heard Kasper's voice in his head. He was eager to learn more about acids and dead bodies, but he was drawing too much attention to himself.

He smiled and said, "No, no. Let's not do that. He's probably busy and I've got things to do, too. I'll just drop the carcasses off at an animal shelter or a crematory. No big deal."

"You sure?"

"Absolutely. You have a nice day, alright?"

"Yeah, you too."

Max went to the checkout counter and bought his goods. He shared no more than a mutual greeting with the cashier before splitting ways.

'How are you today?'

'Fine, thank you.'

Then Max went to the grocery store on the first floor and bought himself a bottle of vinegar. As if he were going through déjà vu, he had the same conversation with the grocery store's cashier.

'How are you today?'

'Fine, thank you.'

Max managed to keep a low profile. As far as the staff knew, he was just another customer. He looked odd because of his wrinkled clothing, stained hands, and tired eyes, but there were no physical characteristics that separated sadistic killers from regular people. Murderers didn't walk around with horns sticking out of their heads and hooves for feet. Killers were customers, too.

12

THE SMELL

The sound of Max's clacking footsteps and rustling shopping bags echoed through the quiet, empty lobby. It was so quiet that he could hear his sweat brushing his stubble. There were no other guests in sight. One of the receptionists—a young, friendly woman—smiled and nodded at him, then went back to typing on her computer.

Max stopped in the middle of the lobby. He stood still and held his breath, as if the receptionists couldn't see him if he didn't move.

A phone rang about twenty seconds later.

A receptionist answered, "Club Edison Hotel, how may I help you?"

Max hurried to the elevators, as if the phone call were enough to distract both of them. The receptionists looked at him with inquisitive eyes, as if to say: *'What's up with him?'* Max entered an elevator and pressed the button labeled '29.' He leaned back against the wall behind him, loosened his shoulders, and caught his breath.

"Shit, shit, shit," he muttered. "There's no way they didn't notice me. What the hell was I thinking? Goddammit, why did I stop like that?"

Ding!

The elevator reached the 29th floor. He walked out and headed around the corner to his left. He saw the vending machines, ice machine, and the emergency exit. He took a right into the hallway but froze after one step. Silvia Alfaro stood in front of Room 2906—*Max's room*. There was a housekeeping cart in front of her.

"Housekeeping," Silvia announced as she knocked on the door.

The thought of fleeing crossed Max's mind. He took a step back without taking his eyes off the maid and the door to his room. He stopped again. On second thought, he realized he didn't have an escape plan. If Silvia entered his room, the body would be discovered and linked to him. And the hotel had all of his personal information—name, address, phone number, credit card number. He couldn't outrun the police.

He watched helplessly as Silvia knocked on the door again. He was hoping Kasper would answer the door and talk his way out of the situation. But the door remained closed. *He's acting like a hostage,* Max told himself. *He's not going to get himself busted for me. He's probably tying himself up right now.* He understood Kasper's actions, survival of the fittest and whatnot, but it didn't stop him from being annoyed by his absence.

The maid drew the housekeeping staff master keycard from her pocket. Trained to respect the guests' privacy, she knocked one more time.

Just as she reached for the door handle, Max rushed forward and asked, "May I help you?"

"Oh, sorry," Silvia said as she looked back at him. She glanced at the clipboard on her cart. She asked, "Are you Mr. Brooks?"

"Yes, that's me," Max said. He stopped next to his door. Trying to exude confidence, he smirked and said, "But you can call me Max."

"Mr. Brooks, we—"

"*Max*. Really, just call me Max."

Silvia stared deadpan at him, then she nodded and said, "Max, sorry to disturb you so early in the morning. We tried calling your room, but there was no answer."

"What's this about? Is there some sort of emergency?"

"Not an emergency, no. But there have been some complaints about a scent coming from your room, sir."

Max played dumb, narrowing his eyes and jutting his bottom lip out. He looked at his door, then back at Silvia.

"A scent?" he repeated in a wondering tone.

"Yes, sir."

"Well, um... Now that I think of it, I also smelled something. It was a... kind of a... Well, it's difficult to explain without sounding 'crass.' You see, it smelled like... fecal matter and, uh... Well... Maybe some cooked meat or... or rusty metal. It might be coming from another room. Maybe someone ordered room service a couple of days ago and forgot to take their dishes out? And it couldn't have been me because I didn't order room service."

Clasping her hands in front of her groin, Silvia smiled and said, "Sir, I don't think the scent is coming from leftover food or dirty dishes."

"So, you smell it too?"

"I do," Silvia nodded.

"And you think it's coming from my room?"

Silvia bit her lip and lowered her head. She could see through Max's bullshit and she was already growing tired of it, but she was taught to stay calm and respectful around obnoxious guests.

She said, "Yes, sir. The scent is very strong here."

Max tipped his head back and sniffed, like a dog under a dining table. He leaned closer to his door and sniffed again. *Hmm*—he hummed in contemplation. Then he smiled and raised his finger at Silvia—*Aha!*

He said, "I think I know what's going on here. Last night and this morning, I heard someone upstairs flushing their toilet *over* and *over* and *over*. I was going to call the front desk, but I didn't want to embarrass them. I had my headphones on anyway. Busy night working, you know? Anyway, I think they might have clogged their toilet or something. Probably burst a pipe by flushing so much."

Silvia looked at the bag in Max's raised hand. She spotted the scrub and bottle of drain cleaner. Upon noticing her stare, Max lowered his arms and hid the bags behind his legs.

He asked, "Have you even checked upstairs? Have you called any other guests?"

"No, sir, but we've received complaints from other–"

"I'm a member of your loyalty program. Been one for years. Stayed at your hotels all over the place. Spent thousands of dollars on upgrades and breakfast buffets. I don't appreciate you harassing me about a smell that's obviously not coming from my room. I especially don't appreciate it when you come here accusing me of–of–of… *stinking* up the place without any evidence. It's terribly rude. Honestly, it's embarrassing for me and it should be embarrassing for you."

Doe-eyed, Silvia looked up at Max, stunned by his rant. She was trained to deal with difficult guests, but Max was more than just a fussy, stubborn customer. He was erratic and unhinged. The tone of his voice seemed to change with every other word—casual to serious, friendly to hostile, cheerful to furious. It was as if he himself didn't know what he was feeling. The housekeeper moved back, inadvertently pushing the cart away from the door.

She said, "We will check the other rooms and find the smell. If you need us to clean anything, we're available 24/7. You can call us directly or call the front desk to schedule an appointment. The instructions are on the phone. We don't require any tips. Since you're staying in one of our executive suites and you're a valued member of our loyalty program, most cleaning fees are waived. You can call the front desk and find out more about that if you'd like. Um..." She looked at the floor and scratched her hair. She was running through her training in her head. She said, "Oh, and we apologize for any inconvenience we may have caused."

Max said, "I appreciate that. I'm sorry, too. Honestly, that smell is *not* coming from my room. I hope you find the source and... whatever. No hard feelings, okay?"

"Of course. Have a nice day, Mr. Brooks."

Silvia grabbed the cart's handle and did a U-turn in the hallway. She smiled and nodded at Max as she quickly pushed the cart past him. Max watched her until she turned the corner. Even after she vanished from his sight, he kept staring down the hallway. He heard the housekeeping cart roll into an elevator, then he heard the doors close with a *whoosh*. That was his cue.

He cracked his door open a bit so as not to let the awful stench out. He squeezed himself into the room through the narrow gap, then he shut the door behind him.

13

A BAD, BAD MAN

"*Kasper*," Max rasped as he secured the swing bar lock, bags swishing in his hands. "You fucking asshole. You just said we were in this together. You said you were going to stick with me until the end."

The room was cold and quiet. Max swallowed his shout before he could blurt it out. He wanted to yell, kick and scream like a spoiled child at a store, but he couldn't risk disturbing his neighbors. They were already bothered by Katie's stench. Loud noises in the early morning would have only added fuel to the fire.

As he walked to the bathroom, he said, "You left me hanging out there, you selfish dick. She almost opened the damn door. She would have..."

Katie's butchered body was still in the suitcase, but Kasper wasn't in the bathroom. Max stepped into the bedroom. He inspected the room from left to right and then right to left. Kasper wasn't there, either.

"Don't let it get to you," Max whispered as he set

the bags down on the entertainment center. "This happened last time. He's here. I just can't see him because... because... I don't know why, but he's here."

He ambled through the room so he wouldn't miss a thing. He opened the closet. It was empty. He peeked under the bed, like a child checking for the bogeyman before sleep. There was no one there. He checked behind the curtains, then he stood on his tiptoes and checked the narrow ledge outside of the window, as if he expected to find Kasper hanging there.

But no.

Kasper had vanished without a trace.

Max sat at the foot of the bed and stared at the wingback chair. He said, "You were right there last time. You were gone, then you were there. Come back, Kasper. Show yourself."

Five minutes passed. Lemony rays of sunshine entered the room through the gaps around the curtains, moving steadily over his body. Muffled footsteps entered the room from the hallway. The other guests were heading down to the lobby for breakfast.

Max's eyes ached and dried out while his vision doubled and blurred. He didn't blink the entire time. If Kasper was going to appear out of thin air like last time, he wanted to see it. A thick vein protruded from the center of his brow and his head started to tremble.

He closed his eyes and whispered, "Where are you?"

"I'm right here," Kasper said.

Max's eyes flew open. The chairs were empty. He

looked over his shoulder, then back at the chairs. Kasper didn't appear.

"Where?" Max asked. The room was silent for ten seconds. Max yelled, "Where?!"

"I'm here, I'm here, I'm here..."

Max heard Kasper's voice, but only from his left ear. He turned to his left and faced the headboard. No one sat next to him.

Kasper said, "I'm right here, Max."

This time, Max heard him from his right ear. He turned around and looked at the television. He squinted at the television's speakers.

"In–In the TV?" he stuttered.

"Where I've always been."

The voice struck Max's right ear again. He glanced at the foyer of the room. He was positive Kasper's voice was coming from the bathroom. *Did I check the tub?*—he wondered. He slunk through the room, shoulders hunched up to his ears. A terrible fear gripped him, but curiosity pulled him forward. He heard someone rambling incoherently in the bathroom.

"Kasper, is that you?" he asked.

He gasped and teetered back, eyes widening in horror. He caught himself on the closet door. His teeth clattered and knees clapped.

"Wh–Wh–Who are you?" he stammered.

A tall, gaunt man stood in front of the bathroom mirror, his head just a few inches below the ceiling. He was nude, webs of thick veins standing out against his dry, translucent skin. His body was dappled with green and purple spots. Strands of long, withering hair stuck out in thin patches from his balding scalp. There was more hair—gray and wiry—on his crotch than his head. His body was devoid of fat and muscle. Every bone was pronounced. The ridges of his spine were especially sharp and protuberant.

Max could see his pale, hollow face in the mirror. He noticed the man's eyes were gray and glassy. The man's mouth was wide open, revealing his brown and black decaying teeth as well as his bloody, receding gums. He looked like he was already dead—a walking, talking corpse. *A rotting man,* Max thought.

"Bad, bad man," the intruder mumbled without his lips ever meeting. "Bad, bad man. I'm a... bad, bad man."

"What?" Max asked, not loud enough to be heard by anyone but himself.

The Rotting Man shoved his fingers into his gaping mouth. He pinched one of his canines and moved it around. Blood filled the oral vestibule between his lower lip and teeth. The blood overflowed, dripping from his flaky, chapped lip. With a good tug, the tooth popped out of his mouth and fell into the sink. Then he pulled two incisor teeth out at the same time. The teeth bounced in the sink like heated Mexican jumping beans.

He pulled on his upper teeth, moving his entire head with each tug. His gums tore open as another incisor and canine came out. Bubbly goops of blood mixed with saliva fell from his mouth and splatted in the sink. He dug his spindly fingers *into* his gums and started scratching. A burning sensation spread through his mouth, but it seemed to comfort him. He moaned in pleasure, eyes rolling back as blood ran down his hands.

Max stammered, "Wh–Wh–Who... Wha–Wha... Ka–Ka–Kasper, what–what is going on?"

The Rotting Man stopped scratching. Bloody fingers in his mouth, he turned to face Max. Max's heart jumped into his throat. The closet door rattled as he leaned back against it. The Rotting Man was grotesque, his presence was inexplicable and horrifying, but Max couldn't look away. He felt an eerie sense of familiarity. He was drawn to the Rotting Man like drivers attracted to gory pileups.

"Bad, bad man," the Rotting Man mumbled.

"You... You're..."

The Rotting Man squeezed his right eye, driving his fingernails into it, then he pulled on it while grinding his remaining teeth. His extraocular muscles tore, blood outlining his eyelids. Then his eye stretched out of its socket. He groaned and staggered as his eye slid out of his fingers. Part of his eyeball sat on his cheekbone, bulging out of his face. His hip bone *thudded* against the edge of the counter—a direct hit.

Yet, the Rotting Man appeared to welcome the pain. He pinched his right eye and pulled on it again. His fingernails sliced the back of his eye and cut into his retina. Unable to handle the pressure, the optic nerve was severed. He caught his eye in his hand. A couple of squirts of blood came shooting out of his hollowed eye socket. He held his hand out in front of him with the mutilated eye rolling on his palm, as if he were offering it to Max.

"Oh my God!" Max screamed. *"Oh my God!"*

"Max, what the hell are you doing, bud?!"

Wide-eyed, Max turned to his right. Kasper stood beside him, his hand on his shoulder and concern written on his face. Max looked back into the bathroom. The Rotting Man was gone. The bathroom was exactly as he had left it—flooded in blood and toilet water with a slaughtered corpse stuffed in a suitcase. He looked back at Kasper.

"You alright?" Kasper asked. "You look like you've seen a–"

"Don't say it," Max interrupted. He wasn't interested in hearing clichés and he didn't want to even consider the possibility of him seeing a ghost. He took Kasper's hand off his shoulder while glaring at him. He asked, "What did you do to me?"

"What are you talking about?"

"Did you drug me? Did you put something in my drink?"

"Are you serious?"

"What did you do to me, you bastard?"

Kasper snickered, then he said, "Shit, you *are* serious." Max shoved him, launching him back against the entertainment center. Kasper yelled, "What the fuck, man?!"

Max grabbed his shirt and said, "You drugged me, didn't you?"

"You're going to stain my damn shirt, douchebag!"

"You drugged me, didn't you?!"

They glared at each other, then Kasper huffed.

He said, "You wouldn't be in this situation if you'd just stop and think things through. No, I didn't drug you, Max. How would I even do something like that? Hmm? You haven't had anything to drink except tap water. You think I drugged the entire hotel's water system? Do you think I gassed the room? I'm not wearing a gas mask, Max. If I did that, I would have been losing my shit like you, right? So, why don't you tell me your theory so I can debunk it? Go ahead, I'm listening."

Max didn't have any evidence to support his accusations. He only blamed Kasper because he was the only other living person in the room.

He said, "Maybe... Maybe when I was unconscious."

"What? What happened when you were unconscious?"

"You... injected me... with something."

"I came here with no bags, Max," Kasper said. He pulled his pockets inside out to show they were empty. He said, "I have no syringes on me, no pipes, *no drugs*. You can call the cops, too. Tell 'em to bring a sniffer dog. They won't find anything on me or you. They won't find anything in your piss, either, when they're booking you. The truth is: You're not drugged. You're just stressed and tired. Stress does scary things to the mind."

Max let go of him and stepped back. Kasper adjusted his shirt while checking for stains. Max thought about the Rotting Man. The Rotting Man and Kasper weren't in the room at the same time—at least, he didn't *see* them at the same time. So, he couldn't connect them. He focused on Kasper's disappearance instead.

Facing away from Kasper, Max said, "You were gone again."

Kasper pointed at the wingback chair and said, "I was sitting right there."

"Yeah?"

"*Yes*."

"Then why didn't you answer the door when the housekeeper was knocking? Why didn't you come out and help me?"

"You already know the answer to that. How could I open the door for a housekeeper while I'm in here alone? Do you know how bad that would look for me? I'll tell you. It would look like I was *babysitting* this body for you. Actually, they'd probably think *I* killed her at first. So, I was waiting for you. I was thinking of excuses, hoping you would show up to save the day. And you did. I was about to thank you before you accused me of drugging you. And I mean that, Max. You could have walked away, but you didn't. So, I guess I am thanking you after all. Thank you, buddy. Thank you..."

Why does everything he say always makes sense?—Max thought. It was as if Kasper were telling him what he wanted to hear, or perhaps he was *hearing* what he wanted to hear. He didn't trust Kasper, but he didn't trust himself, either. He only knew one thing for certain: The sooner he got rid of the body, the sooner he could go home.

He said, "I'm sorry. I overreacted. The woman, that housekeeper... she just spooked me. That's all."

"Yeah, sure. I understand."

"Can we finish this?"

"I think that's a good idea, Maxie. And I know just how to get started."

14

MAKE HER BLEED

Katie's body hung from the shower curtain rod, arms and legs outstretched above her. Her wrists and ankles were tied to the rod using torn pillowcases and bedsheets. She swung above the bathtub like a chandelier. Her head hung below her torso, her blood-stained hair pointing down at the tub. Her mouth was gaped open and, without her tongue or teeth, the opening of her throat was clearly visible. Her muscles had stiffened, hard as stone, due to the rigor mortis. Blood dripped from the crater on her ass.

"Are you sure about this?" Max asked.

He stood in front of the bathtub in his underwear with his arms crossed, a steak knife in his right hand. Kasper leaned against the doorway, rubbing his chin as if he were contemplating Max's question.

He said, "I think, after everything we've been through, we both know we can't be sure about anything. Neither of us have done this before, right?"

"To be honest with you, I have no idea."

"Okay, okay, we'll deal with the... the twisted dreams and shattered memories later. Now, what we know for sure is: We don't know anything. How about that? But I just *feel* like this is our best option. They do it in slaughterhouses, don't they? They bleed the animal dry. If you do that to her, if you 'drain' her, I'm guessing she will weigh a lot less and she'll be easier to chop up. It should help with the rigor mortis, right?"

"Maybe?" Max shrugged as he examined the corpse.

"That's good enough for me. Go ahead. Make her bleed."

Max took a deep breath. He pressed the serrated edge of the blade against Katie's neck. He paused as thoughts of her family entered his mind. His gaze went to her bumpy face and mangled mouth, then to her fingerless hands, and then to the blood in the bathtub. He thought: *How would they react if they saw her like this? How would they feel if her body was found in pieces? What kind of monster have I become?*

He thrust the knife into her throat. The weight of Katie's dangling head helped him saw through her firm muscles. He sliced her jugular, then severed her trachea, and then cut her other jugular, slashing her neck from ear to ear. He could see reds, whites, and blues in the deep wound, colors like the American flag. He spotted the ridges *inside* her trachea, too.

He expected blood to squirt out of her jugulars in

uncontrollable geysers. Instead, it poured out of the cut in small waves, cascading down Katie's face.

Max took another deep breath as he turned his attention to her arms. The mere appearance of her fingerless hands unnerved him. He thrust the blade at her left wrist, then he dragged it down and followed one of her veins down to the crook of her elbow. He repeated the process with her arteries as well, slicing her vertically across her forearms.

Then he cut her other arm, following her veins with the blade. Each laceration was deep and long. It was a disturbing sight, reminding him of the countless suicides he had witnessed while going down the most depraved rabbit holes on the internet. The blood went down her arms and trickled from her shoulders.

He drew a third breath, long and loud. He grabbed her foot in one hand. Her icy skin made him shudder. He sawed into her ankle until he severed her Achille's tendon. He heard it *pop* as it ruptured. He grabbed her other leg with his free hand, pressing his thumb into her calf muscle, then he cut into her other ankle. Her heel cord snapped and he felt it slither down her leg towards her kneepit.

Max looked down at the tub. He watched as ribbons of blood swirled down the drain. It wasn't much, but even a drop was enough to sicken him.

"Is... Is that good enough?" he asked as he stepped back.

Kasper said, "It's definitely not bad. *But,* it's almost

check-out time. You need to make her bleed as fast as possible. Stab her back a couple of times."

"O–Okay."

He crouched and leaned forward, knees against the edge of the bathtub. He thrust the knife up at Katie's back. He exhaled each time the blade penetrated her body. He started at the small of her back and made his way up to her shoulders. He stabbed her fifteen times along the way. Most were deep enough to cut her organs while some were superficial. Her pierced kidney and lungs bled the most. The leaking blood sounded like big drops of rain hitting an umbrella.

Max looked back at Kasper and asked, "How about now?"

Kasper said, "Perfect. Let's give her a couple of minutes to bleed out. Come on, let's have a seat in the bedroom." Max didn't move. Kasper beckoned to him and said, "Seriously, you need a breather. Let's sit."

Kasper walked away, but Max didn't hear his footsteps. He couldn't remember if he had ever heard him walking through the room. *He's light-footed,* he told himself as he sought a reasonable explanation. *I mean, I haven't noticed my own footsteps tonight either, have I?* He shrugged off the thoughts and followed Kasper into the bedroom. He didn't want to stay in the bathroom out of fear of seeing the Rotting Man again anyway. He found Kasper sitting on a wingback chair with one leg crossed over the other.

Max sat on the foot of the bed across from him.

They were quiet, like a couple of shy kids meeting for the first time.

Kasper smiled and said, "Okay. What's on your mind?"

"What's that supposed to mean?"

"You clearly want to say something, so say it. I'm listening. Look at me like a... like your therapist. Yeah, that should help. I'm your therapist. What's on your mind, kid?"

Max couldn't tell if he was being facetious or sincere. There was a lot on his mind. He was disturbed by the night of murder and mutilation. He was troubled by his nightmares and visions, too. *Where do I begin?*—he thought.

He said, "I've been thinking a lot about what I've done, what I *may* have done, what I've seen, and what I *may* have seen. I think it's obvious by now that I've gone mad. This—all of this—is madness. Maybe I'm sick in the head. Or maybe you're right. Maybe it's the stress and the guilt." He smiled but his face was devoid of happiness. He said, "I know I'm going to be haunted by guilt for the rest of my life."

"I won't sugarcoat it. I think you're right, Max. This night, it's going to affect me in the same way. I can already feel it. The guilt, the shame, *the filthiness*. It's all running through my veins. So, how do I get it out? Hmm? Do I cut my wrists and let it out that way? Should we kill ourselves?"

"Huh? No. I mean... I don't know. You think we should do... *that?*"

"Would you?"

Max asked, "Would I kill myself?" Kasper nodded. Max said, "I don't... I'm not sure that would solve anything. I probably deserve to die, but I think her family or their families would rather see me behind bars. If it comes to that, then it is what it is. Are you, um... Kasper, are you thinking about killing yourself?"

Kasper stared at him with a blank, emotionless face. He looked like he was sleeping with his eyes open. Max thought about waving his hand in his face or snapping his fingers next to his ear. Then Kasper smirked.

He said, "No, I'm not. Just thinking about how we're going to get out of this."

"Listen, I'm sorry for dragging you into this. I know we've had our differences tonight, I've lost my temper more than once, but I really am sorry. I hope you realize that."

"It's fine. I'm your friend, Max. We're like brothers for crying out loud. I'll *always* be around for you."

Max sniffled and said, "I'll make this right. If anything goes wrong, I'll do whatever I can to protect you. This was all my–"

A loud groan interrupted him. Puzzled, they looked at the foyer of the room. A second groan came from the bathroom.

Max whispered, "The Rotting Man?"

Kasper said, "Shit, it's not going to hol–"

A *snapping* sound echoed through the room, quickly followed by a booming *bang* and crunching *thud*. The men ran to the bathroom. The shower curtain rod couldn't handle the corpse's weight. It snapped in half, sending Katie plummeting to the bathtub.

Kasper said, "Ah, shit. I knew she was tall, but she didn't look *that* heavy."

"Someone must have heard that. There's no way someone didn't hear it. It sounded like a damn explosion."

"Let's not be too negative here. It's possible that none of your neighbors are in their rooms right now, so maybe no one heard a thing."

"I get that you're trying to be optimistic, but this isn't the time for that."

Kasper said, "I know. It's time for you to start chopping up that body."

"*Now?* What if someone complains? What if the housekeeper comes back?"

"Then you deal with that when it happens—*if* it happens. What else are you going to do? Wait here and waste your precious time? Just start cutting her into pieces. While you do that, you think of some excuses for the housekeeper or anyone else who might show up. That should keep you distracted and make this easier for you, right?"

Max looked at the body, then at the door. He counted each passing second, waiting for the housekeeper or manager to knock. *One, two, three, four, five, six, seven, eight, nine, ten*—ten seconds passed without a peep from the hallway. He pushed past Kasper and grabbed the box of garbage bags from the entertainment center, then he barreled back into the bathroom.

Max rolled Katie onto her stomach in the bathtub. He grabbed the cleaver from the counter and held it over his shoulder, ready to swing it at her but not sure where to begin.

Noticing his hesitation, Kasper said, "Start small. For practice, you know? Look at her feet, Max. It wouldn't take much to cut 'em off now, would it?"

Max glanced at her feet, then he frowned, looked away, and lowered the cleaver. The torn pillowcase used to tie her legs to the rod had slid *into* the wounds on her ankles, causing the cuts to widen. Fragments of her broken bones protruded from the gashes. Her feet were barely attached to her legs. He let out a shuddery sigh before turning to face her lower body.

He gritted his teeth and swung the cleaver at her left ankle. The blade *clanged* off her lateral malleolus—the outer bone of her ankle joint. He swung it down again, sending a dull *thud* through the hotel room. While swinging it up, a splash of blood flew off the blade and splattered on the wall. He grunted as he swung it a third time, putting his weight behind it.

Her left foot was lopped off. The toes hit the bathtub first, then it tipped over and rolled. It moved, tilting like a seesaw for a few seconds. Her blood didn't spray out from the stump at the end of her leg like it did in the movies. Only a couple of drops trickled out.

Pride glimmering in his eyes, like a father watching his son's dreams come true, Kasper said, "I knew you could do it."

Max made an 'O' with his mouth and puffed out another trembling sigh. Kasper's words of encouragement didn't help.

"I can do this, I can do this, I can do this," he whispered.

He swung the cleaver at Katie's other ankle. It cracked her fibula bone. He met some resistance while trying to pull the blade out. He shook it while tugging on it. Then he stumbled back and landed inside the luggage as the blade slid out. He grabbed the edge of the bathtub and pulled himself up to a crouch. He groaned as he chopped away at her ankle.

Clang!
Thud!
Clang!
Thud!

It took seven chops to break her bones, shred her muscle, and tear through the ligaments and tendons. Once amputated, the foot hit the wall of the tub, then slid down towards the other severed extremity.

Kasper said, "So far, so good. Why don't you..."

Before he could finish, Max straightened her left arm out beside her. He straddled the edge of the tub, one foot planted outside of the bathtub and the other inside of it. He swung the cleaver at her wrist until the blade *clanked* against the tub and he dismembered her hand. He did the same to her other hand—chopped it off at the wrist.

As he collected the amputated extremities and stuffed them into a garbage bag, he said, "Sorry. I was just tired of seeing her hands like that."

From the doorway, Kasper said, "No need to apologize. Initiative's a good thing."

Max threw the garbage bag between the toilet and the bathtub. He asked, "What's next?"

"The easy stuff is out of the way. I think it would be best if you just tackled the hardest part. If you made her... less than human."

"Less than human?"

"I'm saying you should behead her. It's going to be difficult, but if you take her head off, you'd reduce her to an unidentifiable body—a slab of meat. Now, I'm not the one getting my hands bloody, but I'm assuming that would make things easier for you."

"Yeah, I get what you're saying. So, I just... I chop her neck with this?"

"Yup."

"Okay, okay. Sure. I can do it."

Max bent forward and grabbed a fistful of her hair. He felt the dried blood on her blonde locks crumbling between his fingers. He struck the nape of her neck with the cleaver. Her spinal cord cracked. He twisted the handle to widen the wound and separate the cervical vertebrae. He yanked it out, then he swung it down at her again.

He groaned and whined with each chop, repulsed with himself. Sweat ran out of his wild hair and down his cheeks. His hand and wrist started to ache from all the chopping. It took him five minutes to reach the center of her throat. He pressed the back of his hand against his mouth, burped, and then hiccupped as he fought the urge to vomit. He leaned back against the wall behind him to catch his breath.

Beheadings were tiring.

Max could see the inside of Katie's throat. He saw her torn muscles and tubular esophagus. A gurgling sound came from somewhere on her neck. He couldn't tell if it was coming from her slit larynx or her severed esophagus. Through the blood, he could see the colors *in* her neck ranged from salmon-pink to crimson and light blue to purple.

He gripped her hair again and started cutting. Her head moved with each chop. The blood swirling down the drain under her face helped her head glide. The massive wounds on her neck helped, too. Max imagined he could turn her head 180 degrees. After another five minutes, her head was only attached to her body by some strands of muscle. He tugged on her hair and swung at the last bit of flesh.

He pulled her head off. His elbow hit the wall behind him with a loud thud. A tingly sensation surged through his arm and he let go of the head.

"Shit," he muttered as he rubbed his injured elbow.

Kasper asked, "You okay?"

Max said, "Yeah, just…"

He closed his eyes and gasped. He had spotted Katie's head rolling from side to side in the tub. The fact that he had been beheading someone didn't really sink in until he finally completed the act.

Eyes closed, he asked, "What am I doing, Kasper? How the hell did I get here?"

Max's eyes flung open as someone knocked on the door. Before he could ask for help, he realized Kasper was already gone. He grabbed Katie's head and put it in the garbage bag with her hands and feet. He stumbled over to the sink and washed his hands and face vigorously. Someone knocked again.

"Open the door, asshole!" a man yelled from the hallway.

As he rushed to the closet, Max shouted, "Give me a minute, please!"

"Goddammit!"

Max grabbed the bathrobe from the closet, tossed it on, and tied it. He checked his reflection on the vanity mirror as the man knocked again. He leaned forward and checked the bedroom. He couldn't find Kasper and he didn't have time to check under the bed or behind the curtains. He reached for the door handle, but he stopped before he could touch it. He closed the bathroom door, then he checked his hands again.

In the hallway, the man yelled, "If you don't open this goddamn door right this second, I'm calling the–"

Max cracked the door open and peeked out into the hallway. Huffing and puffing, Gary Stokes stood in front of his door. He was a burly middle-aged man.

"What is it?" Max asked.

"What is it?" Gary repeated, voice stern with anger. "You've been making noise all night and all morning. What the hell are you doing in there? Chopping wood? Banging on the damn walls?"

"I–I'm sorry. I must have had the volume on the TV higher than I thought. I sleep with earplugs, you see, so I don't notice sometimes."

"The TV? *Bullshit*. I heard it from your walls. I could feel them shaking, you little punk."

"Then maybe it was the pipes."

"Pipes?! Jesus Christ. You are an asshole, aren't you? Maybe I'll call the front desk and tell them about 'the pipes.' Maybe I should call the cops, too. What do you think about that, smart-ass?"

Max said, "I'm sorry if that came out the wrong way. I wasn't trying to disrespect you. It's just that I really don't know what you're talking about. I was sleeping, okay? If the noise came from my room, I apologize and I promise it won't happen again."

Gary's nose wrinkled upon catching a whiff of the rancid odor in Max's room. He pushed the door, as if he were invited to enter. Max put his foot behind the door and anchored himself against the wall to his right. The men glared at one another.

Gary said, "I knew that smell was coming from your room."

"What smell?" Max asked, face tightening into an expression of anger and fear.

Gary laughed inwardly, then he asked, "What do you got in there? Dead animals? A dead body?"

Max's face turned to stone. The voice at the back of his head said: '*He knows. Kill him.*' He thought about stabbing him through the heart right there in the hallway.

Trying to bottle his anger, he said, "If you must know, I've been having some 'digestive issues' because of some spicy curry I ate for dinner last night. If you'd like to come in to examine my *shit*, all you have to do is ask."

Max clenched his jaw and exhaled through his nose. He wanted to slap himself. Instead of defusing the situation, his anger got the best of him. He felt stupid for provoking the man.

Gary said, "You're a liar. If I wasn't here with my family, I would have..." He leaned in closer to the door. As if he were afraid someone might hear him, he hissed, "I would have fucked you up already, you little douche. I'm calling the front desk. And I'm not asking for a housekeeper or a bellboy, I'm bringing the manager up here. And I'll be here when they come so I can see your face get stupider than it already is."

Max bit his tongue to stop himself from lashing out at him. He looked him up and down. He noticed his fists were clenched so tight that his knuckles turned white. Gary watched him with narrowed eyes, waiting for him to say something—waiting for him to give him a reason to hurt him. The man had a bad temper, especially when his family wasn't around.

Yet, Max stayed quiet. He wasn't going to take the bait. Gary snarled and shook his head, then he marched away. Max poked his head out of the hotel room and watched him. Gary entered the neighboring room—*Room 2904.*

"No, no, no, no, no," Max muttered. "I'm fucked."

15

DESPERATE MEASURES

Max secured the locks on the door. He gasped and turned around as the closet slid open. Kasper stepped out, eyes on his Rolex.

"When'd you go in there?" Max asked. "You–You weren't in there when I–I grabbed this bathrobe."

Kasper responded, "Don't start with that again. I told you I was going to hide in the closet when that asshole started knocking. *I* handed you that bathrobe."

"N–No, that's not how it–"

"Listen, Max, we don't have time for this. We can expect another housekeeper to show up in a couple of minutes. If not, then the manager will be on his way. But that's a good thing. Managers are always busy, so that might buy us thirty minutes or an hour. They might even wait until check-out time to confront you. But, even in the best-case scenario, that doesn't give us a lot of time. So, get in there and start chopping."

"B–B–But–"

"Get your ass in there and start chopping!"

Max winced, rattled by Kasper's shout. He heard the frustration in his voice. *I'm annoying him,* he thought. *This is all my fault and I'm just making things worse.*

"I'm sorry, Kasper," he said.

"Don't apologize. *Chop.*"

Max nodded and said, "I will. I will."

He took off his bathrobe, letting it fall to the floor in front of the door, then he entered the bathroom. He grabbed the cleaver and sat on the edge of the tub. He hadn't noticed it until that moment, but squirts of blood had been spraying out of what remained of the corpse's neck after the grisly decapitation. Her blood showered his bare foot.

He turned the dead body on its side. The mere glimpse of her mangled chest sent shivers down his spine. He pulled her left arm overhead—over-*neck*—towards him and the bathtub faucet, then he rolled her back onto her stomach. He chopped her shoulder with the cleaver, the blade *clanging* and her bones *thudding* each time.

The blade broke her scapula, humerus, and even clavicle. It ruptured her bursa—the fluid-filled sac *inside* her shoulder. While chopping, he jerked her stiff arm around to help stretch and widen the wound. He could see the torn muscles, broken bones, and severed ligaments in the deep, jagged gash. He angled the blade and started sawing towards her armpit with it.

It took him about four minutes to amputate her arm.

Max tried to fold her arm over like a flip phone, but the rigor mortis stopped him. He thought about asking Kasper for help, but he already knew the answer: *No!* So, he stepped on her forearm and pulled on her upper arm while swinging the cleaver at the crook of her elbow. Her arm was thin, so it only took five chops to cut it in half. He threw the pieces into the suitcase.

While cutting her other arm at the shoulder, Max said, "What are... my chances... of getting... out alive?"

"Very high, actually," Kasper said. "Even if you get caught with her body, as long as you don't run at the police with one of those knives, they're not going to shoot you."

Max wiped the blood and sweat off his brow with the back of his hand, then he continued chopping and said, "I asked... the wrong question. What are my chances... of getting out of here... without handcuffs?"

"As long as you stop hesitating, I'd say they're pretty good."

"Stop hesitating," Max whispered to himself.

"Confidence is key, my friend. Don't forget that."

"Confidence is key..."

Max picked up the pace, the blade *whooshing* with each swift swing. By the time he had amputated her right arm, his entire upper body was covered in her blood. He tried swiping the blood off his face, but he was just smearing it at that point. And he wasn't done yet. He proceeded to cut her arm in half at the elbow. He threw the pieces into the luggage.

He scooted along the edge of the bathtub until he reached the center of it. He planted the heel of his foot in the crater on her ass cheek—to pin her down and to block his view of the wound.

He swung the cleaver at her upper thigh, directly below the curve of her ass. Her legs were thicker than her arms, but he managed to cut through her muscles. The femur was durable, though. It was the longest, strongest bone in the human body.

Unable to break it, he took the cleaver out and forced the steak knife into the gash. He used the serrated edge to saw through the muscles around her femur bone. Blood jetted out as he cut her femoral artery. Then he switched his stance, holding the knife in the icepick grip like a serial killer in a horror movie. He thrust the knife at the femur bone, chipping away at it to weaken it.

While stabbing the bone, he stomped on her thigh —stab, stomp, stab, stomp, stab, *stomp*. The bone broke. He cut the rest of her muscle with the steak knife to amputate her leg, then he used the cleaver to cut her leg in half at the knee. The heavy pieces landed with *thumps* inside the luggage. He went to work on her other leg.

From the doorway, Kasper watched with a mix of concern and anticipation in his eyes, like a man witnessing his wife give birth to their child. Dead body disposal was a tricky, risky art form. And like an audience member watching a dangerous magic trick, the same questions swirled in his mind: *Will he survive? Can he escape? Can he make her disappear?* The room was ripe with tension.

After severing her right leg and cutting it in half, Max threw the slabs of meat into the suitcase. Exhausted, his legs wobbled as he stood up. He climbed out of the bathtub, slipping and sliding because of his bloody feet. He grabbed four plastic bags and started stuffing the limbs into them—two pieces in each. One bag had a forearm and a thigh, another had an upper arm and a lower leg.

He tied each bag and stacked them next to the toilet. He returned to the bathtub and towered over the corpse's torso. His arms easily slid under her abdomen thanks to the blood. He groaned as he lifted her up. He carefully stepped out of the tub and lowered her trunk into the suitcase—belly-down. The corpse fit perfectly.

He put the five bags of human parts in the suitcase. Two of them fit above her neck and shoulders. He squeezed the other two between her ribs and the sides of the suitcase. He put the last bag—filled with an upper arm and a lower leg—on her back. He closed the suitcase, bags rustling inside, but he couldn't zip it shut.

Max muttered, "Oh shit, we were so close. We were almost finished."

"It's okay. It's good enough like that."

"But it won't close."

"Then take one of the bags out and carry it on top

of your suitcase while you're rolling it out of here. Like a duffel bag, you know?"

"But what if–"

"If anyone asks, you tell 'em it's laundry. But, unless there's a cop out there, no one's going to ask. Think about it. Has a hotel employee ever asked you what you're packing?"

"N–No, they haven't."

"Exactly. You have nothing to worry about."

Max took the bag on the corpse out of the luggage. He zipped up the suitcase, then he lifted it into an upright position. Although it was black, blood and toilet water glistened on its hard exterior. He put the bag on top of the handle. Kasper stepped aside as Max rolled the suitcase out of the bathroom. He left it standing next to the front door.

He took off his underwear, then he stumbled back into the bathroom and turned on the shower. The leftover bodily fluids and chips of bone went down the drain. He climbed into the bathtub and washed the blood off himself.

While lathering his body with soap, he asked, "What's the escape plan?"

Kasper returned to the doorway and said, "I was thinking you'd check-out, then walk out through the front doors. Same as everyone else."

"Then what?"

"We split ways. You hide your 'luggage' and think of a way to fix this—to get your life back in order. And if you get caught on the way and all of this unravels, you make sure you tell 'em you threatened to kill me if I went to the police."

"Can you help me find somewhere to hide... *her?*"

"I'll think of some options before you check-out, but once you leave this hotel... I think that's where we say goodbye for a while."

Max stopped scrubbing himself. He wondered if Kasper was planning on ending their friendship *permanently* or if he was just being cautious by suggesting they distance themselves from one another *temporarily*. He had taken Kasper to the depths of his madness. He couldn't blame him for not wanting to be friends with a deranged killer. He would have done the same if he were in Kasper's shoes.

After shampooing his hair, he turned the showerhead and sprayed the bathroom floor. Waves of bloody water rippled towards the doorway. Max stepped out of the bathtub while drying himself with a towel. He put on his bathrobe and joined Kasper in the bedroom. Calm and collected, Kasper was already sitting on one of the wingback chairs.

Max grabbed his pants from the entertainment center and looked through his pockets. He found his wallet. He checked all of the pockets on his coat, then he checked the pocket on his shirt. They were all empty. His heartbeat thrummed in his ears, fast and loud. He pulled his pockets inside-out. He found nothing but lint.

"What are you looking for?" Kasper asked.

Max stopped rifling through his clothes. He stared down at his pants and said, "I can't find my keys."

"Which keys?"

"My–My car key. My house key. *My keys*, man, they're not here."

"Did you even have them to begin with?"

Max turned to face him and asked, "What do you mean? Of course I did. I–I drove..."

He stopped—a dramatic pause—and looked at the floor. He remembered killing Katie, but he couldn't remember driving to the hotel. An image of himself sitting in the backseat of a sedan flashed in his mind. His eyes swiveled in their sockets. An episode of lightheadedness pushed him against the entertainment center.

He said, "No. No, I–I *didn't* drive here. I came in a taxi... in an Uber... because I didn't want anyone to see my car. Yeah, I planned this all out." He dropped to his knees and absently gazed at the carpet. He said, "I don't understand myself. Why the hell did I think I drove here?"

Kasper shrugged and said, "Beats me."

"Beats me?" Max repeated. He glared at Kasper, stunned by his casual demeanor. He crawled over to his seat, then knelt at his feet and clasped his hands in front of his chest. He said, "I know you said you can't get involved, but I need you now more than ever. Please, Kasper, I'm begging you. Let me use your car to get out of here. If we get caught, I promise I'll tell everyone that I threatened to kill you. I'll hold a knife up to your neck if we get pulled over. *Please*."

"I can't do that."

"Come on, man! I'm on my knees here!" Max snarled without unclenching his teeth.

"Max, I *can't* do that!"

"Why the hell not, man?!"

"Because I didn't drive here, either! You know that already!"

A long, tense silence befell the room.

Max leaned away from the seat and sat on his heels while staring up at Kasper in awe. Kasper's words echoed in his head. He understood his first sentence, but the second one bewildered him. '*You know that already!*' It begged a question that he was afraid to ask. But his sanity had already crumbled. He had nothing to lose and everything to gain.

He said, "How did you get here?"

Kasper grinned and said, "You really are something else, Maxie."

"Answer me."

Kasper muttered, "What a shitshow... But sure, why not?" He leaned forward, elbows on his knees, and said, "You see, I can't drive you out of here because I came here... *with you*. We came to the Club Edison Hotel in the same Uber at the same time."

"No. I called you here after I... killed her. You were late, remember?"

"Max, isn't it about time you–"

The phone rang.

Max said, "Shit, that's them."

Kasper grabbed Max's robe at the chest and pulled him up to his feet. He yelled, "You have to leave! They're coming!"

"I can't! I still have to clean the room!"

"Forget it! It's too late for that now! Run, Max!"

"I can't! They'll catch me!"

Max closed his eyes, put his hands over his ears, and screamed in agony. The phone's ringing was high-pitched, unusually sharp and loud. He felt the sound waves crawling in his skull. He scratched his scalp and pulled his hair, trying to dig the noise out of his head.

"Look at me," Kasper said as he shook him. Max could hardly hear him over the ringing. Kasper yelled, "Look at me!"

"Help me!" Max cried as he opened his eyes.

"You have to go, Max. You don't have time for another meltdown. Grab the suitcase and run."

"I can't just run out of here! Why don't you understand that?! They're coming! They'll see me!"

"Buy time. Go next door. Pay your neighbor a visit, then sneak out once the staff gets in here and the chaos begins."

Max stammered, "I–I can't... He–He won't... You–You... You, Kasper, you–you're..." He looked down at himself and touched his bathrobe. He stuttered, "I–I'm not even dressed. I'm not... Oh God, I can't do this!"

"Do it, Max! Do it!"

The phone rang again and again—and again *and again*. It now sounded like a hundred phones were ringing simultaneously. Yet, under the ear-splitting screeching, he could hear Kasper's voice hitting him from every angle. '*Do it. Do it. Do it.*' He recognized the voice from his vision of his fiancé's murder.

Index fingers buried in his ears, woozy and disoriented, he lurched away from Kasper. His stomach churned and his throat swelled. He felt the floor rocking under him and walls revolving around him. As if it were attached to a bungee cord, the ceiling flew up, plummeted towards him, then rose again.

Max knew it wasn't real, it was all a product of his madness, but it still frightened him. So, his survival instincts told him to run and protect himself. He slid into the bathroom and grabbed the boning knife from the counter. He was curious about Kasper, but he was too scared to look back. *Every man for himself,* he thought.

Wearing only his bathrobe, he rolled his suitcase out of the room and kicked the door shut behind him.

16

THY NEIGHBOR'S KEEPER

MAX STOOD MOTIONLESS IN THE HALLWAY. THE LOUD ringing stopped immediately after he closed the door. An uneasy silence followed—as quiet as a buried corpse. The corridor was vacant, not a soul in sight or a peep from his neighbors. His headache and nausea subsided, the screeching in his ears ended, and he regained his balance.

He leaned in close to the door and whispered, "Kasper. Kasper, are you in there?" There was no reply. He said, "If you're in there, if you can hear me, I'm going to do it. I'm getting out of here."

Once again, there was no response.

Dragging the luggage behind him, Max moved towards the neighboring room—Room 2904. The suitcase's wheels *clunked* and *thudded* while the garbage bag on top *crinkled*. The silence made it sound louder than normal, as if a train were speeding down a rusty track in the hallway. He stopped in front of the door.

Just as he raised his fist to knock, he spotted the bloody wheel tracks on the carpet. The tracks started at his room and led directly to Room 2904. *'You don't want to make it easy for the police.'*—He heard Kasper's voice in his head. He looked to his left, then to his right, then back to his left. There was no one around to see him, but there were security cameras at the ends of the hallway.

He dragged the suitcase to Room 2902, then to 2901, then to 2903, and then back across the hall to 2904. He left a trail of bloody, zigzagging tracks behind him.

Max knocked on the door, then put his thumb over the peephole. Most mindful people checked their surroundings before answering their doors, but he hoped Gary's anger would cloud his wisdom. He needed him to make a mistake—the worst mistake of his life. He heard footsteps and a muffled voice on the other side of the door. He knocked again, striking the door as hard as possible.

"I'm going to see who it is, alright?" Gary hollered. As he pulled the door open, he said, "What the hell... are you..."

His voice softened until it was muted. He recognized Max from their confrontation earlier. He wasn't intimidated by him, he was sure he could beat him in a fistfight, but he was worried about the knife in his hand. Like a cornered animal, there was a scared, desperate look in his eyes, too. And desperation often led to rash, dangerous behavior.

Gary said, "Hey, now. If you want to–"

Max lunged forward and thrust the knife at his neck. Gary leaned back to dodge him, but he wasn't fast enough. It all happened in what felt like a nanosecond.

The blade cut through his Adam's apple and pierced his larynx. He ground his teeth and gripped his neck with both hands, as if he were strangling himself. Blood flooded his windpipe and dripped into his lungs. He coughed up a red mist while gasping for air. The blood flowed out from under his hands, too, pouring down to his chest and soaking his white t-shirt.

Max rammed Gary's chest with his shoulder, forcing him to stumble back into the room. The bag fell off his suitcase as he pulled it through the doorway.

"Oh my goodness," a woman gasped from the bedroom.

Gary responded with a pained croak.

Max tried to shut the door, but the severed limbs stopped it from closing. He slammed the door three times before he noticed the garbage bag. It had torn open, the upper arm protruding from a hole. He dragged the bag into the room, then he closed and locked the door. He heard footsteps and whimpers in the bedroom—*panic*.

"God, no, please," the woman cried.

Max made his way past the bathroom and emerged in the bedroom. There was an entertainment center to his right, two beds to his left, and a round table surrounded by two chairs at the end of the room.

Hands around his neck, Gary had collapsed between the two beds. Amy, his wife, knelt with Gary's head on her legs, rocking back and forth in shock. Their children, Daniel and Kylie, lay on the farthest bed from the entrance. Daniel, an eleven-year-old boy, propped himself up on his elbows and watched Max— eyes wide with fear. Kylie slept with her back to the commotion, unaware of the violent intruder in their hotel room.

Amy's heart sank upon noticing Max. Her face crumpled with dread and revulsion and anger and sadness. They didn't move, eyes locked like a pair of cowboys in a duel. Max shook his head slowly, communicating without saying a word: *'Don't do anything stupid.'* Amy sobbed while Gary gargled his own blood and Daniel panted as he stared at his dying father while Kylie purred in her sleep.

Amy turned and grabbed the phone from the nightstand behind her. She thrust her finger at the '9' key to call the police, but she missed and hit the '7' and '8' keys at the same time.

Max rushed towards her. He pointed the knife at her, but he was aware of a mother's natural selflessness. Amy was willing to sacrifice everything for her family. She was ready to die to protect her kids. So, Max pointed the knife at Daniel in order to gain some leverage over Amy. The boy grimaced and cried. He peed himself, soaking his pajama pants and the blanket.

"Mo–Mo–Mommy," he whined, his voice shrill and trembling.

Kylie continued sleeping beside him. Gary snorted, his left leg shaking uncontrollably. Amy lowered the phone back to its cradle while holding a hand out between her son and the intruder.

In a soft voice, so as not to awaken her daughter or alarm her son, she said, "Please don't hurt us. Take anything you want. My wallet, Gary's..." She paused to lick her lips and breathe, then she said, "My husband's wallet, it's on the table behind you. Take it and go. I promise I won't tell anyone you were here."

Max said, "I don't want to hurt you. I didn't want any of this, okay? I just need... I need everyone to be absolutely quiet. I'll leave in a minute. That's all I need. One goddamn minute. Okay?"

Amy wasn't stupid. Her husband was bleeding out on her lap and Max was holding a bloody knife. She could see he was unstable and dangerous. She couldn't believe a word out of his mouth. But she couldn't fight him, either. She was stuck under her husband. She feared she couldn't overpower him in a fair fight anyway.

She stuttered, "Ca–Can I call 911?"

"What? *No*. Of course you can't."

"Please, sir, please. He needs an ambulance or he'll–"

"Just stay quiet for a minute. I'm going to check the door. If the coast is clear, I'll leave. It's that easy, okay?"

"Okay, okay. Just go check the door already. *Please*. He–He's..."

She glanced over at her son. She had never seen him so pale—*so scared*—before. She refused to amplify his fear by admitting his father was dying.

"He needs help," she said.

"*A minute,*" Max responded sternly. "Okay?"

Amy forced a tight-lipped smile and nodded at him, bottling her anger and frustration. Max retreated, his feet barely rising from the floor as he walked backwards. He kept his eyes—and his knife—on the Stokes family until he reached the foyer of the room.

As soon as Max vanished around the corner, Amy turned towards her son and whispered, "*Shh, s–shh. Baby, give me your pillow.*"

Daniel stared at the foyer of the room. Through the reflection on the vanity mirror, he could see Max standing next to the suitcase near the front door. And he saw the amputated arm sticking out of the garbage bag.

Raising her voice but not yelling, Amy said, "Daniel, please. Give me your pillow. Your daddy needs it."

Daniel finally looked at his father. The man's eyes were closed, but his mouth was wide open. The boy understood the concept of death, he knew all about danger, but he never experienced it first-hand. This was his first time facing his mortality as well as his family's. He couldn't move. He could tremble and whine, but *he could not move.*

Amy pulled the pillow out from under him. She took the pillowcase off, then she slid out from beneath Gary. She put the pillow under his head and the pillowcase over his hands.

"It's okay, hun," she said softly. "I've got you. I'm going to put pressure on it. Let me put pressure on it, sweetie. Pl–Please, I have to do this."

Gary couldn't see her. He knew he was in the hotel room, but he couldn't remember where he had landed. He couldn't even remember who had stabbed him. At the brink of death, memories came in flashes. He was thinking about the time he took his family to Chuck E. Cheese to celebrate Daniel's eighth birthday. It would have brought a smile to his face if he wasn't in so much pain.

But he recognized his wife's voice and it calmed him. He trusted her with his life—always did. He moved his hands. A squirt of blood flew out of the wound, missing Amy's chin by a centimeter. It splatted on his face. For a second, she saw the white of his thyroid cartilage in his wound. She held the pillowcase over the cut to slow the bleeding.

While Amy tended to her husband's wound, Max walked in circles near the front door and ran through his options in his head. He wasn't expecting to get away with murder, but he didn't want to get arrested at the hotel. He had to discover Andrea's fate. He had to see her with his own two eyes. So, a hostage situation was out of the question.

A pair of footsteps in the hallway interrupted his

thoughts.

Max looked through the peephole. He saw Kasper pacing back and forth in front of the door. He appeared to be saying something.

"What are you doing out there, man?" Max muttered. He glanced back to check on the Stokes family. Amy was preoccupied with Gary and Daniel was paralyzed with fear. As he opened the door, Max said, "Kasper, asshole, you're going to lead 'em right to..."

Kasper was gone.

Max stuck his head out of the room. He looked to his right. There was no one down the hall. The only noise came from the vending machines, humming like refrigerators in a convenience store. Then he looked to his left. Wearing a suit, the manager—an older gentleman with white hair and a matching mustache—stood next to a housekeeper and her handy cart in front of Room 2906.

Max quietly closed the door and fastened the locks. Beads of cold sweat ran down his face and neck, and his breathing intensified into raspy wheezing. He put his hand on his chest, as if he feared his heart were about to explode. He dragged his feet to the bedroom where he found Amy with the phone in her hand.

"You stupid bitch," he growled as he ran towards her.

"Help!" Amy cried before she even finished dialing.

Nine, one...

Max stepped over Gary and thrust the knife at

Amy's face. It went through her cheek and sliced her tongue, disrupting her shriek. He tore a two-inch gash into her cheek as he yanked it out. He stabbed her face again. The tip of the blade hit her cheekbone, taking a chip off it, then the blade slid towards the bridge of her nose. Blood poured out of the cut and filled the black bag under her left eye.

"Stop!" Daniel cried. "Don't! Stop! S–Stop! Don't hurt my mom!"

Kylie awoke, startled by her mother's bloodcurdling scream and her brother's shouting. Bug-eyed, she sat up in bed beside Daniel. She couldn't see her incapacitated father from that angle, but she could see the intruder violently stabbing her mother. She joined her brother in weeping hysterically.

Amy grabbed Max's forearms to stop him from stabbing her a third time. So, Max slammed his knee against her sliced face. Her teeth clanked, her cheekbone cracked, and the cut under her eye widened and stretched. He kneed her again for good measure. Dazed, her limp hands fell from his arms. She leaned against the nightstand.

Max thrust the knife at her face and neck. The blade skewered her left cheek a second time. It cut her trapezius muscle next to the collar of her shirt, then it nicked her neck. It cut her ear in half horizontally, but both pieces remained attached to her head. Blood entered her ear and muffled her hearing. Yet, she could still hear her children crying. It hurt her more than the vicious stabbing.

The blade sliced her scalp three times, cut her forehead open horizontally, then it slid *under* her scalp. He wiggled the knife, lifting her scalp from her skull until he could see the bone under the bush of hair and bloody flesh. While Amy screamed and rasped, Max thrust the knife at her face again. The blade cut her jaw before snapping in half.

As it turned out, human skulls were stronger than cheap kitchen knives.

But Max wasn't done with her. He was consumed by his bloodlust. He grabbed a handful of her hair and pulled her away from the nightstand. While doing so, a large chunk of her scalp came off her skull, causing her to squeal. Most of her face—from her forehead down to her left cheek—was covered in blood.

"Let her go!" Daniel cried. He leapt to the foot of the bed and grabbed Max's arm. He yelled, "Stop! Stop it! Don't hurt her!"

"Stop!" Kylie cried as she covered her ears with her hands and shut her eyes.

"Let her go! Mom, no! Please don't–"

Max turned and struck Daniel's face with his elbow. One of Daniel's upper incisor teeth broke. He fell back, blood gushing out of his nose. Kylie didn't notice. With her eyes closed, she kept begging Max to release her mother. Max dragged Amy into the bathroom. He pushed her to the floor face first, then he picked her up and forced her to stand on her knees. Holding two fistfuls of her hair, he swung her head at the counter to their left.

Amy's temple collided with the edge of the counter. Upon impact, splashes of blood flew from her head and splattered on the sink, wall, and mirror. She was knocked unconscious.

Max released her hair and let her hit the floor. He marched back into the bedroom. Like his mother, Daniel was out cold.

Kylie's vocabulary was reduced to four words: *Mommy! Daddy! Stop! Help!*

Max grabbed Gary's ankles and dragged him away from the beds. Gary reached for the mattress, bloodied fingers gliding across the bedsheets. His hands slid over Daniel's legs, then over one of the bed's legs. He was too weak to get a grip on anything. He couldn't stop Max from taking him away from his children. As they entered the foyer of the room, someone knocked on the front door.

"Is everything okay in there?" a man asked from the hallway. "Hello? Excuse me, I'm the manager. Sir? Ma'am? *Hello?*"

The manager knocked again. Max ignored him and hauled Gary into the bathroom, leaving him next to Amy. A *beep* and *click* came from the foyer as the manager tapped his master keycard on the door's lock. The door swung open a few inches before the swing lock stopped it. The manager and the housekeeper could hear Kylie's cries from the hallway. The manager tackled the door—once, *twice*—but he couldn't break the lock.

He closed the door, then he turned towards the

housekeeper and said, "Wait here. I'm going to get Michael and the cops."

"What am I supposed to–"

"Just call me if anyone comes out!" the manager yelled as he hurried to the elevators. "And don't touch anything!"

In the bathroom, Max opened the sink cabinet and took a hair dryer out. He plugged it into the socket next to the mirror and turned it on. The hair dryer roared, drowning out Kylie's cries. He turned it up to its maximum heat—nearly 200 degrees Fahrenheit. Amy regained consciousness. She pushed herself up to her hands and knees, arms and legs shaking.

Max huffed, then he said, "You bitch... You *stupid* bitch. I asked you for *one* minute! One *fucking* minute! Look at what you made me do! Look at what I have to do because of you!"

Amy stuttered, "Da–Daniel... Kylie... Ba–Baby..."

With a tug of her hair, Max pulled her head up to his crotch. On her knees, Amy mauled his forearms, clawing at his skin with her sharp fingernails.

She yelled, "Help! Help us!"

As she screamed, Max shoved the barrel of the hair dryer into her mouth. He pushed it as deep as possible, her teeth scraping the barrel. The hot air dried her throat and filled her lungs. She felt an unusual pressure in her ears. And that pressure quickly turned into pain—sharp, burning, *deafening* pain. She dug her fingernails into Max's arms first, then she grabbed the hair dryer's handle, and then she scratched her neck.

She had options—turn off the hair dryer, pull on the cord to unplug it, hit Max's testicles—but she didn't consider any of them. Panic opened the door to chaos in her head, flooding her mind with irrational thoughts. *Cut a hole into your neck, it'll help you breathe!* She flailed against the cupboard while scratching her neck and kicking at Max's shins, then she fell to her side and thrashed about beside her husband.

Max took a step back and watched her. Blood spread across the whites of her eyes, surrounding her blue irises from every angle. A droplet of blood came out of her left ear. A few seconds later, a drop oozed out of her other ear. Her bulging jugulars appeared to be slithering in her neck. Thick veins protruded from her forehead. Her hands dropped to her inflating chest. Over her shirt, she clawed at her breasts while absently gazing at the ceiling.

"*One minute!*" Max yelled. "Why couldn't you give me one goddamn minute?!"

He grabbed the chest of Gary's shirt and lifted his upper body from the floor. The man was barely awake, skin ashen and mottled blue due to his severe loss of blood and lack of oxygen. He slammed Gary's head against the rim of the toilet bowl. His skull and the bowl cracked at the same time. Then he dunked Gary's head into the toilet water.

Gary resisted, bloody water sloshing around his shaking head. He grabbed the rim of the toilet bowl and pushed himself up. Max put his knee on Gary's back and grabbed the back of his head with both hands. He used his entire body to keep his head submerged in the toilet water. He felt Gary's back vibrating under his knee and he saw the man's arms trembling. After twenty seconds, Gary's arms went limp and he stopped moving.

But Max didn't take his hands off him. The killer inside of him told him to make sure he was dead. A muffled *popping* sound surprised him. He glanced back at Amy. Her chest was inflated with the small of her back arched and her arms down to her sides. He couldn't see it, but her lungs had burst. Blood was now coming out of the corners of her eyes, ears, nose, and mouth. Her eyes were wide open, but she was already dead.

Max staggered off Gary. He turned off the hair dryer. A *hissing* sound came from Amy's body. He squinted at her nose, then at her ears, searching for the source to no avail. He exited the bathroom. The front door was closed. He expected to find the manager as well as an army of security guards and cops waiting for him in the hallway. He heard a footstep. He looked to his left and found Kylie staring at him, holding a stuffed dog against her chest.

Teeth chattering, she stammered, "M–Mo–Mommy?"

What would Kasper do? Max asked himself. *He'd kill her. He'd kill them all. No witnesses, no evidence, no case.* If Kasper were there, he would have been able to convince Max to kill the children. But Kasper wasn't around and Max couldn't convince himself to do it. The devil on his shoulder was gone.

He closed the bathroom door behind him and said, "Go to bed."

"Mommy?" Kylie repeated, sniveling and shuddering.

"Go to bed, honey. Your mom... She'll be with you in a minute. She's... She's taking care of daddy, okay?"

Kylie stared at the intruder for fifteen long, uninterrupted seconds, then she rushed back to the bed. She shook her brother's shoulder and tried to wake him.

Max looked through the peephole. He saw the housekeeper's cart to his left, but he didn't see the maid or the manager. He searched the foyer of the room for a weapon. *Break the mirror and use a shard as a knife?* He didn't want to rely on a weapon that could easily break in his hand. *Whip them with a coat hanger?* Coat hangers were often used as tools of abuse, but they weren't very effective against adults.

His eyes lit up as he stared at the garbage bag on top of his suitcase. He took the upper arm out from the hole on the bag. It weighed a little less than five pounds, but it was stiff and durable. He swung it in front of him like a club. Blood splattered on the door. He swung it again to get used to it. More blood hit the door.

"Just like a hammer," he said. "I can still do this. I can get out of here."

17

ESCAPE FROM THE CLUB EDISON HOTEL

The housekeeper, Isabel Fierro, chewed on her fingernail while staring at the door to Room 2904. The hair drier had stopped her from hearing the violent murders in the bathroom and the children's cries. She could only hear footsteps, soft voices, and feeble whimpers now. She looked over her shoulder. Another guest, Warren Valentine, stood outside of Room 2909 with a cell phone in his hand—ready to call the police and record the scene for a viral video. He had heard the commotion from his room and he had been speaking to Isabel about it.

Warren asked, "You still hear 'em?"

"A little," Isabel said in a hushed tone. "I don't know, maybe it's not them. Could be a TV or something."

"You hear from your boss?"

"Not yet. He said he was going to get Michael and the cops, but that could take a while."

"Why? Who's Michael?"

Isabel said, "He's the security manager, but I think he had a meeting with the police today. The other guy's been here for a week. And the other one was late today. I'm not even sure if he's here yet."

Warren shrugged and said, "Listen, I heard those kids crying, too. It sounded real serious. If you want me to help you bust that door down, I can give it a try. I'm not really trying to get into any trouble, though."

"Yeah, I just don't know what to..."

Her voice trailed off as she heard the *click* of a lock. She slowly turned her head to face the door. Her eyes big and wet, she interlocked her fingers in front of her chest and drew back upon hearing the *clank* of the swing lock. The door was pulled open. The bloody suitcase was pushed out of the room. Eyes growing and pupils dilating, she saw the severed leg through the hole in the garbage bag.

Max exited the room behind his suitcase. He stopped in front of the door and stared at the housekeeper. He couldn't see her through the peephole, but he wasn't surprised to find her in the hallway. He wasn't expecting another guest, though. Barely moving his head, his gaze went back and forth between Isabel and Warren.

Warren put his hands on his hips and watched Max with a furrowed brow from down the hall. He couldn't see the bloodied suitcase, the severed limb in the garbage bag, or the amputated arm in Max's hand over the housekeeper's cart. Isabel froze up. She had seen some awful things in her time as a housekeeper—domestic abuse, diarrhea-stained bathrooms, bloody bedsheets, baby puke smeared on walls—but she had never seen a man carrying a human arm before.

Max swung Katie's arm at her. It *clapped* against her cheek and knocked her back. Her feet tangled and she fell to the floor.

"*Hey!*" Warren shouted as he rushed towards them. Max lurched away from the housekeeper's cart, dragging the suitcase behind him. Warren yelled, "Stop! Hey, stop it, man!"

He stopped next to the downed housekeeper. He noticed the blood smeared on her cheek, but he didn't spot any cuts. He took a step away from her, ready to give chase, but then he noticed the bloody wheel tracks and the amputated arm in Max's hand.

"No fucking way," he said.

Good Samaritans had their limits. They were happy to help stranded drivers and the elderly across roads, but they couldn't be expected to chase down killers who used their victims' body parts as weapons. He went back and helped Isabel up to her feet.

Max called an elevator. There were three elevators in front of him and three behind him. He walked in circles, checking each light to see which one was going to arrive while frequently glancing at the hallway around the corner.

Ding!

A set of doors opened behind him. He stumbled into the elevator, pressed the '1' button, and then pounded the *DOOR CLOSE* button five times, as if that would speed it up. As soon as the doors closed, he fell back against the wall behind him and caught his breath. He watched the numbers above the doors illuminate one by one, dropping as the elevator descended.

28, 27, 26, 25, 24...

He whispered, "Don't stop. Please don't stop."

He held the amputated arm like a baseball bat. He felt his racing pulse in his fingers and an uncomfortable warmth in his legs.

16, 15, 14 ,13, 12...

On the elevator door's reflection, he spotted the surveillance camera above him. He looked up at it, then back at the doors. He had almost forgotten about the cameras.

4, 3, 2, 1.

Ding!

The elevator arrived at the first floor. The doors slid open. Max gasped as Kasper barged into the elevator. Horrified, he sprawled himself back against the wall behind him.

"What are you doing here?" Max asked quickly, words jumbled together.

Kasper marched up to him, leaving only six inches of space between them. He said, "You're in trouble."

"No shit!"

"Keep your voice down," Kasper hissed as the

doors closed behind him. "I'm trying to help you, you idiot."

"You've been fucking with me all night."

"That's a lie," Kasper said as he wagged his finger at Max's face. "A *fucking* lie. I've risked everything to help you. I could have walked out on you and called the police a long time ago, but I stuck around and I guided you through this. You wouldn't have gotten this far if it weren't for me."

"This far?" Max repeated in disbelief. "What are you talking about, man? Look at me. I'm running around in a bathrobe with a suitcase full of body parts and a... a..."

He frowned at the amputated arm in his hand, as if he had finally noticed the depravity of his actions. He was worse than a killer. He was a maniac.

Kasper said, "You're almost out of this, Maxie. You're so close to the finish line. While you were in the other room 'taking care' of our neighbors, I was cleaning up your mess. I left it almost *spotless*. Traces of her blood might still be around, but *our* DNA is gone. Then I snuck out while the housekeeper was distracted. Now, I could have walked out the front door a while ago, but I *knew* you'd show up here and I *knew* you'd still want to get out of this. I couldn't let you make a mistake."

"Wha–What mistake? What are you talking about?"

"I know what you're thinking. Run out, hail a cab, go home. You've given up on getting away from this, haven't you?"

"Ha–How did you know that?"

Kasper said, "You can't give up now. You have to find the security room and sabotage the hotel's surveillance system. If you can do that, you can escape with your freedom."

Max shook his head and said, "No, it's impossible."

"It's possible."

"I killed three people. Maybe more, Kasper."

"And you did it so you can get away from this. Don't let them die in vain. Don't become a cold-blooded killer. Get into the security room and get rid of the footage."

Max kept shaking his head. His eyes were empty—so empty that it looked like he was sleeping with them open or looking right through Kasper and seeing nothing.

Kasper leaned closer to his ear and said, "I did my part. I told you how to get rid of her body. I cleaned the room. Trust me one more time and I promise you'll go home to your fiancé so you can start rebuilding your life. And if you won't do this for yourself, do it for me and the victims. You can't help anyone from behind bars, can you?"

Max felt like he was hearing Kasper's voice *inside* his head, words ricocheting off the walls of his skull like bullets off pavement. And, like a charismatic politician, Kasper was convincing. Max couldn't tell if it was the calm, soothing tone of his voice or his friendly, nonchalant attitude, but he just couldn't resist him.

He said, "I don't know how to find 'the security room' or even delete the footage. I'll need your help."

"I'm going to be in the lobby. I'll keep a lookout and, if the police show up, I'll distract them. Think of me as your last line of defense. As for the security room, you already know where to find it—behind the reception desk. There's probably a receptionist there, maybe two, maybe the manager. They have keycards around their necks. Get your hands on one and you're in."

"What if they don't–"

"You don't have time for what-ifs. Let's go."

"But–"

"*Let's go.*"

Max sighed and pressed the DOOR OPEN button. He got out of the elevator, pulling the suitcase behind him.

Walking beside him, Kasper whispered, "And remember, you can't leave any witnesses. Kill everyone who makes eye contact."

"*What?* You just said I can't become a cold-blooded–"

"It's the only way. I'll be right there in the lobby with you. We're in this together. Good luck, Maxie."

"Kasper, I can't just…"

Kasper walked away. He stopped in the middle of the lobby and took a cell phone out of his pocket. He flicked his thumb across the screen and muttered to himself, acting like he was searching for something.

His stare darted to the elevators. He beckoned at Max with an inconspicuous swing of his head.

Max went down a wide corridor, the suitcase's wheels *clattering* behind him. The wheels stained the marble floor with blood. He emerged in the lobby with a human limb in his hand, bringing a coppery stench with him. Morning sunshine poured into the lobby through the tall windows, illuminating every corner of the room. Vehicles sped down the street outside, but there were no cops in sight.

"Oh my God," a young brunette woman gasped from a seat in front of the reception desk. She uncrossed her legs and lowered her cellphone. Face contorted with disgust and horror, she yelled, "Oh my God!"

She grabbed her duffel bag from the floor as she stumbled off her seat. She ran past two other women in the lobby. They followed her, running out while looking back at Max. One of them abandoned her luggage.

"Holy shit," an older, roly-poly man muttered from the hotel's entrance.

He grabbed his luggage and hurried out while dialing 911 on his cell phone. The guests scattered in the parking lot. The brunette woman stopped to warn an arriving family.

'*Don't go in there! There's a psychopath inside!*'

Max approached the reception desk. One of the receptionists—a blonde woman—screamed as she ran away. The other receptionist, Kayla Lane, was paralyzed with fear. They had heard about the troublesome guest on the 29th floor, but nothing could have prepared them for Max's appearance in the lobby at that moment.

Max saw the door behind Kayla, the keycard around her neck, and the keycard lock above the door's handle. The sign on the door read: *EMPLOYEES ONLY*.

On the verge of tears, he wagged Katie's arm at her and said, "Don't look at me. Don't look at me!" Kayla lowered her head and raised her hands, as if she were being held at gunpoint. Max said, "Don't make this hard. You... Just give me your key and get out of my way."

"O–Okay," Kayla stuttered. "Ta–Take whatever you want."

"Your key! Just give it to me and go!"

"Okay, okay!"

Just as Kayla grabbed her neck strap, the door behind her swung open. The manager stood in the doorway. The name tag clinging to his coat read: *Jim Hamond*. They stared at each other in a moment of tense silence.

Kasper yelled, "Get in there, Max!"

His scream echoed through the lobby, but Jim and Kayla didn't react. Max vaulted over the desk. Kayla shrieked at the top of her lungs. Jim grabbed her arm and pulled her into the room. Before he could close the door, Max tackled it, knocking them both back. Kayla scrambled around a desk while Jim struggled to his feet.

Max found himself in a small office. There were three short aisles of desks in front of him. Two desks hugged the wall next to the door behind him. A door on the parallel wall led to the employee break room. To his left, he could see a wall of monitors through an open doorway—*the security room*. Each monitor showed a different room or hallway in the building. The room looked empty.

Jim leaned against a rolling chair to regain his balance. He held his hand up to Max and said, "Don't do this. The cops are on their way."

"I don't care," Max responded. He pointed the limb at the security room, although it looked like he was aiming it at Jim. He said, "Just look away and let me into that room."

Kayla wedged herself into the corner of the room, sitting on the floor with her hands cupped over her mouth.

Jim said, "We can handle this calmly."

"We can! I know that already!" Max yelled, desperate for his cooperation. "Just stop looking at me and everything will be fine!"

"Sir, please. We all have families. Just step away and–"

"Damn it, just stop looking at me!"

From behind him, Kasper said, "It's too late. He's seen too much. He can identify you. Kill him."

Max cried, "No, not yet. Don't talk like that. I can still do this. I don't have to kill him."

"Excuse me?" Jim responded with his brow raised.

Kasper said, "There's no way around this. Do it, Max. Save us."

"I can't keep killing people," Max whined.

"You have to. For Andrea, for me, for yourself."

"I can't!" Max yelled as he looked back at the doorway.

His heart skipped a beat. He felt every drop of blood in his body freeze. To his astonishment, Kasper wasn't there. He heard a footstep in front of him. He turned to find Jim rushing towards him. Jim grabbed Max's robe at the chest and pushed him back towards the door. He had tried to tackle him to the floor, but he was too weak to take him down. They crashed into the wall beside the door.

Jim pressed his cheek against Max's chest, wrapped his arms around him, and started pulling him down. Max dropped the limb. He had to sacrifice his weapon to stop the manager from gaining the upper hand. He grabbed the doorway in one hand and the neighboring desk in the other. He clenched his teeth together as he pushed himself up.

Max launched his knee up at Jim's stomach, knocking the wind out of him. Jim fell to one knee, picked himself up, then his face landed against Max's abdomen and untied his bathrobe. His genitals hanging out in the open, Max pushed Jim back against a desk, which caused it to hit the neighboring desk and then that one hit another one.

The desks rattled and groaned. A wireless keyboard fell off one of the desks. A computer mouse hung from another one. And a folder slid off the table at the end.

From the corner, Kayla yelled, "Stop it! Jim, no! No!"

Jim moaned and squirmed against the desk. Jolts of pain surged from the small of his back. Max gripped his neck with both hands and pushed him, bending him backward over the table. He heard some of his bones *pop*.

"I told you to stop looking at me!" Max shouted.

Frothy saliva sprayed out from between Jim's teeth. He grabbed Max's wrists first and tried to pry his hands off his neck, but Max just tightened his grip. So, he slapped the desk behind him and reached for the closest weapon. A cheap ballpoint pen rolled into his hand. He thrust it at Max's chest like a knife. The pen's barrel snapped in half along with its ink chamber.

The black ink drenched Max's chest and Jim's hand. The pen couldn't penetrate his firm chest, but he was hit with enough force to drive him back.

Grunting, Jim stood straight and rubbed his lower back. Max ran back at him. He tackled him, slamming him back against the desk. The monitor flew off the table, hit the rolling chair, then plummeted to the floor. He clutched Jim in a bear hug, lifted him up, and then slammed him on the floor. Jim's right shoulder shattered with a crunch. A long, ghoulish groan, like a zombie's in a horror movie, escaped his mouth.

"Fuck you!" Max yelled as he punted his face.

He yelped and lifted his right knee up. He had

broken his big toe on Jim's chin while also knocking the manager unconscious for ten seconds. While bouncing on his good foot, Max searched for another way to hurt him. He was drawn to the paper shredder attached to the small trash can to his right. He hauled Jim over to the trash can. He dipped the man's fingers into the paper feeder slot, but it didn't activate. Jim didn't notice. He was conscious but groggy.

Max grabbed a sheet of paper from the neighboring desk. He put the paper into the slot first. The machine started buzzing. He raised Jim's arm up from the floor, then he fed his fingers into the slot in front of the paper. Jim bellowed as the tiny blades tore his fingertips apart and broke his fingernails. His blood splattered on the sheet of paper and dripped into the trash can through the slot. The trash can shook as the paper shredder stopped with a loud crunch.

Max pulled Jim's hand out. The blades had whittled his bones and shaved his fingers down halfway to the joints closest to his fingertips. Broken bones and shredded ligaments stuck out from his fingertips. Along with the crumpled paper, cracked fingernails and flaps of skin were trapped between the paper shredder's blades. Blood ran down Jim's hand and arm, soaking the cuff of his sleeve. His head went limp for a second as he nodded off. He regained consciousness, then he dozed off again.

The fingertips, as well as the forehead, were the most sensitive parts of the body when it came to pain.

His agony was unbearable. The burning pain spread from his mutilated fingers to his chest.

Max heard the footsteps on the other side of the desk. Kayla sprinted to the exit. Max ran into her, their bodies clashing just a meter away from the door. Kayla landed on top of a desk while Max staggered back. He grabbed the amputated arm from the floor and struck her face with it as she pushed herself off the table. She collapsed in front of him, stunned but awake. Katie's blood was smeared all over her face.

"Help!" she cried as she scrambled around Max's legs.

"Stop!" Max yelled.

He struck the back of her head with Katie's arm, sending her sprawling across the floor. She got up on her hands and knees, but the arm *thudded* against the back of her head again. Her face bounced off the floor. Yet, she remained awake. She crawled forward on her stomach, inching towards the door. Then she was knocked out with a third blow.

But, despite neutralizing her, Max kept hammering away at her head with the limb. Four, five, *six*—with the sixth blow, her scalp was ripped open. Blood fountained out of the gash.

"Stop!" Jim shouted as he wrapped his arms around Max.

Max yelled, "Get off me!"

He swung the limb back at Jim, but he couldn't reach him. Max crashed into the desk. The monitor tipped over and some drawers slid open. The arm slid out of his hand and landed next to Kayla. Max grabbed a fountain pen from the desk. He thrust it at Jim's arms. The sharp tip couldn't penetrate his sleeves. He leaned back while Jim leaned forward. The old man was weak, but he was still heavy.

Max planted his foot on the edge of the desk, then he kicked himself off it. The men teetered back until Jim crashed into the table behind him, aggravating his injured back.

"Damn you!" Max yelled.

He turned and stabbed Jim's neck with the pen five times. Blood bubbled out of the holes, although he missed his jugulars. The nib snapped off with the fifth stab, trapped in the manager's throat. Jim covered his neck with his hands and tottered away. After about five steps, his legs gave out and he dropped to the floor.

"I would have let you go if you just let *me* go!" Max sobbed. "None of this had to happen! But you people always make me do this! This is your fault!"

He grabbed a sheet of paper from a desk, then he gripped a handful of Jim's thin hair and lifted his head from the floor. He caressed Jim's hands with the edge of the paper, searching for a route to his neck. He couldn't squeeze it past his pudgy fingers. He moved the paper up, tickling his chin, then his lips, and then his nose.

He stopped at the bridge of his nose, then he tilted the paper until it slid between his flickering eyelids. He pressed the edge of the paper directly against his eyeball.

"Ahh," Jim moaned in pain. "Don–Don't–"

Max pulled the sheet of paper, swiping it against his eye. Jim's eye was slashed open horizontally—*a grisly papercut*. The manager drew a long, raspy breath. A string of thick, gelatinous fluid—contaminated with blood—hung from his sliced eye, like mucus from a child's nose. He rolled onto his back with his hands over his eye, weeping and rocking.

Max took another sheet of paper off the desk and straddled Jim's chest. He swiped the edge of the paper against Jim's neck. Jim felt the paper slice him, but the pain was minuscule compared to the throbbing agony radiating from his eye. A droplet of blood came out of the thin papercut on his neck. The paper sliced him two more times before Max crushed it in his hand.

He couldn't slit his throat and sever his jugulars with a sheet of paper—not under those conditions. He shoved the paper into Jim's mouth as he stood up.

As Jim coughed and groaned, Max said, "I just wanted to go home, you bastard."

He stomped on Jim's neck, his heel sinking *into* his throat. Jim's larynx and esophagus were crushed while his spine was broken. He died instantly.

Max picked up Katie's arm and towered over Kayla. He heard the faint wail of sirens approaching the hotel —an army of cops. He swung the arm at Kayla's head. The *thud* of each blow echoed through the lobby. Kayla's legs shook as her skull cracked and her brain hemorrhaged. After a minute, her skull caved in. Her scalp plunged into her head. Bits of her brain came out of her scalp and outlined the sunken shards of her skull.

He heard the emergency sirens in front of the hotel—as clear as the voices in his head. He dropped the amputated arm on Kayla's back, then he shambled into the security room. He was tired—tired of the death, tired of the sadistic violence, tired of the noise. He examined the wall of monitors. Two monitors depicted the hallway on the 29th floor. Jim had been observing the situation prior to Max's intrusion.

In the live footage, the doors to rooms 2906 and 2904 were open. A security guard was hunched over in the hallway, coughing and puking. Another guard stood near him. He carried Daniel's unconscious body in his arms while Kylie stood near them, clenching the guard's pants in one hand and her stuffed dog in the other.

The security guard held a cell phone up to his ear, updating the police on the situation while taking care of the children. A different monitor showed a pair of employees hiding in the machine room behind the elevators.

Three monitors showed live footage of the lobby. He could see flashing red and blue lights as well as people moving outside. It looked like cops were lining up near the entrance, preparing to enter the building. Kasper wasn't in the lobby. He didn't see him on any of the other monitors, either. He noticed one of the cameras was recording the neighboring office. He saw Kayla's dead body and Jim's legs.

He felt a set of eyes on him, as if someone were leering at him. He looked at the doorway and sighed shakily. Kasper stood in the office, smirking.

"What's the matter, buddy?" he asked. Max looked at the monitor. There was no one there. Kasper said, "It's finally hitting you, isn't it? You're not getting out of this. Too little, too late."

Max swallowed the lump in his throat. Shameless, he approached Kasper with his bathrobe open down the middle. He looked back into the security room. He only saw himself and the dead bodies on the monitor.

Teary-eyed, he sniffled and asked, "You're not real, are you?"

"I'm standing right here, aren't I? You can see me, can't you?"

"I see you, but the cameras don't. No one else sees you, r–right?"

"What does it matter? If you see me, then I'm real to you. Even *I* think I'm real sometimes. Like I'm my *own* person, you know? Seriously, who cares what other people *see* and *don't* see. It's like caring about what they're thinking about and what they're *not* thinking about."

They heard a patter of footsteps in the lobby.

"Clear!" a man shouted.

Max said, "I need you to tell me the truth. Did I kill Andrea? Did I... Did I kill my baby?"

Kasper shrugged and said, "If I'm being honest, I can't really remember." He twirled his finger near his temple and said, "It's a little foggy up there."

"You... You bastard."

"Hands up! *Hands up!*" a male police officer yelled from the doorway, aiming his pistol at Max. "Don't reach for anything, motherfucker!"

Without taking his eyes off Max, the cop informed his partners about the suspect and the dead bodies.

Max gazed into Kasper's eyes and asked, "Have you always been fake?"

"Fake?" Kasper repeated. "That's hurtful. I'm your friend, Maxie."

"You–You're not my friend. You... You're imaginary or you're... you're me."

"Well, you know what they say: 'A man's best friend is himself.' It's just a little more... 'true' for some people."

Police officers barked orders at Max from the doorway: *'Hands up! Turn around! Get on your knees! Don't reach for anything!'*

Max said, "So, if I die... you die?"

Kasper huffed, then he said, "Don't get your hopes up, Maxie. You're not dying today. We're going to spend the rest of our lives together in a maximum-security prison. I personally didn't want it to end this way, but what can I do?"

"You can't do anything, but I can still–"

A cop shot him with a stun gun from the doorway. Max's limbs stiffened as he came crashing down to the floor. He ground his teeth and groaned. He saw the cops running around Kasper. Within seconds, four police officers were on top of him. One knelt on the back of his head, another knelt on his back, and the other two handcuffed him.

The last thing he saw was Kasper's arrogant smile before passing out.

18

BREAKING NEWS

FABIANA SANTOS STOOD IN THE PARKING LOT OF THE Club Edison Hotel, holding a microphone in her hand. A pack of bloodthirsty reporters surrounded the yellow tape and police cruisers cordoning off the building. The yellow tape read: *DO NOT CROSS*. Beat cops kept them at bay while forensic specialists and homicide detectives examined the crime scene.

The hotel had been evacuated through the emergency exits. Some of the guests loitered in the parking lot, waiting for answers as well as the opportunity to return to their rooms.

Near a police cruiser, a cameraman stood on his tiptoes to get a better view of the valet area in front of the hotel's entrance. A young cop, Nick Taylor, puked in a bush while a peer poured water on the back of his head. Nick looked shaken and ill, face devoid of color. He had witnessed gory car accidents and violent attacks, but he had never seen a woman's dismembered body stuffed in a suitcase before.

"Good evening, everybody, I'm Fabiana Santos with Channel 7 News," Fabiana said, starting her report with a wide smile of sincere enthusiasm. She effortlessly twisted her face into an expression of concern. She said, "Bleak news today from the Club Edison Hotel where a man, Max Baker, is suspected of gruesomely murdering five people, including guests and employees. Although the suspect is in custody, homicide detectives still have the hotel cordoned off as they speak to witnesses and comb through surveillance footage."

The report cut to footage of Katie—face blurred—in the lobby and elevator of the hotel.

Fabiana continued, "Deputies say Baker's rampage began last night with the visit of a female acquaintance. Police accuse the suspect of murdering the young woman and then attempting to dispose of her body in the hotel. Our sources say the body was dismembered beyond recognition and hidden in the suspect's suitcase. Baker is also accused of attacking a family in the room next to his as well as a hotel receptionist and a manager."

The report switched to footage of Max in the hotel and the neighboring department store. A video of Max, dressed in a bathrobe and talking to himself in an elevator, played on loop.

"Our sources shared this footage of the suspect

with us and deputies have confirmed its authenticity," Fabiana said. "Eyewitnesses claim to have seen the suspect acting erratically throughout the night. Chilling surveillance footage shows him speaking to himself, attempting to hide in plain sight, and wandering the hotel in a trance-like state. Guests on the 29th floor also reported a foul odor coming from the suspect's room. The hotel staff has declined to comment on the incident but have vowed to support the police in their investigation and have also sent their condolences to the victims."

The report returned to Fabiana in the hotel's parking lot. The cameraman zoomed in on the crying friends and family members of the victims.

Tragedy helped retain viewership.

Fabiana said, "During his arrest, witnesses report hearing Baker scream about an accomplice and his fiancé. Deputies have confirmed that they are looking into his fiancé's whereabouts, but they do not believe Baker had any help committing these crimes. He has been taken to a hospital where he's expected to receive treatment for some minor injuries as well as a psychiatric evaluation. If you have any information regarding the suspect, his fiancé, or his victims, the sheriff's department would like to hear from you."

The smile crept back onto her face before the report jumped back to the looping footage of Max in the elevator. In the video, Max kept looking up at the surveillance camera behind him. Despite the pixelization, his expression of fear and discomfort was obvious. The report ended and cut straight into a commercial full of happy actors advertising a cruise.

Tragedy also helped companies sell happiness to sad audiences.

JOIN THE MAILING LIST

That was quite a night at the Club Edison Hotel, wasn't it? Hallucinations and mutilations and desecrations. *Dead Body Disposal* is a standalone novel, but I often write about the human body in my horror novels. If you enjoyed this book's themes, tone, and storytelling, you should know that I regularly publish compelling horror novels. I like to push the boundaries with my work. Psychological, revenge, slasher, supernatural, cannibal, serial killer, coming-of-age, body horror—I've explored nearly every horror subgenre through my writing. (I might even be working on a splatterpunk sci-fi book in the near future...)

If you'd like to learn more about my books and stay up to date with my latest releases, I *highly* suggest signing up for my mailing list. By signing up, you'll also ensure that you won't miss any of my *huge* book sales. (I host some of the best deals of the year—*every year*.) I usually send one email a month, but you might receive two or three during busier months or none at all if I have nothing going on. I won't spam you with blog posts or life updates or my political views. This newsletter is strictly about *my books*. Best of all, it's completely free. Visit this link to sign-up: http://eepurl.com/bNlıCP.

DEAR READER

I think of myself as a designer of death. I've published over *45 novels* featuring hundreds of murders—some more intricate than others. Some characters were killed with firearms, others were murdered with eating utensils. Some were disemboweled, others were beheaded. Some were immolated, others were drowned. My characters have died everywhere from their homes—trailers, apartments, houses, mansions—to the Amazon Rainforest. My point is: I've designed *hundreds* of death and torture scenes throughout my career. *Dead Body Disposal* was spawned by a question that popped into my head one night in early 2020.

What happens to the dead bodies in your stories, Mr. Athan?

(Okay, no, I don't really refer to myself using my pen name.)

This got me thinking about, you guessed it, dead body disposal. I had written hundreds of deaths, I've written a few scenes where the killers disposed of the corpses, but I never really dove into this scenario. So, I started asking myself how would *I* get rid of a dead body. I immediately thought about the Breaking Bad episode '*Cats in the Bag...*' and disqualified that scenario. I didn't want to make it easy for my main character. That's not to say melting a corpse with hydrofluoric acid in a bathtub would be simple, but the setting didn't give me much to work with. I had to raise the stakes. That was when the next question hit me.

How would you get rid of a dead body from the top of a busy hotel?

I placed the main character in what felt like the most difficult yet realistic situation I could imagine. After all, we've all heard the horror stories of people being assaulted or murdered in certain hotels. Regarding the actual process of disposing the dead body, I brainstormed some ideas of my own and I even asked my wife what she would do in this situation. (She spent years working in hotels in Japan and she's a fan of grotesque horror. You already know I love her.) Then I found real cases that supported my outline to add a layer of realism.

The references to the Canadian student found in the water tank atop a hotel, the elderly Japanese woman found in a suitcase in a coin locker, and the woman who was flayed and flushed down a toilet in Mexico... All real. The attempted cannibalism might have been a little over-the-top, but I wanted to showcase an extreme level of desperation. Besides, I did quite a bit of research for that scene (including some deep web studies), so I didn't want to discard it and forget about it. People swallow evidence all the time anyway, right?

You might have a couple of questions regarding the twist at the end. I mean, it's clear that John Kasper was part of Max Baker all along, but you probably have *other* questions, such as: *Is Max a serial killer? Did he really murder Jay Jones in the alleyway? Is Andrea dead?* I left these questions open to allow *you* to freely decipher and/or interpret the book. The Rotting Man might be the most difficult vision to interpret. A part of me wishes I could have dedicated more chapters to that character, but I didn't want to spoil it and I certainly didn't want you to mistake this book for a supernatural story. So, just to be clear: There is *nothing* supernatural in this novel.

This book was a little different for me. I'd still argue that it was one of my most brutal novels—I debated censoring Andrea's death scene for weeks after writing it—but it also explored many different themes and characters. I hope you enjoyed this experience. If you did, please take a moment to leave an honest review on Amazon. Reviews on Goodreads, Bookbub, Twitter, and your blogs and YouTube channels are also appreciated.

Need help writing your review? Try answering questions like these: *Did you enjoy the book? Were you captivated by the characters? Were you satisfied with the ending? How would you get rid of a dead body on the 29th floor of a hotel?* (Okay, answering that last question *might* land you on some lists. But I am genuinely interested in how you would do it.) Good or bad, your reviews help me grow as a writer and help other readers find my books.

I'm writing this letter on November 12, 2020. Not much has changed since my last life update in my letter in *Bad Decisions*—my previous book for those of you who may have missed it. Well, there was an election back in the United States. As of now, I'm glad it hasn't exploded into violence. I continue to hope for the best for my home country, although I'm still living in Japan. The pandemic isn't too bad here and I'm hearing talks of a vaccine. Once things get better, I hope to attend horror conventions and finally ship out autographed copies of my books. For now, I'm focusing on my work. I'm working overtime to deliver my best lineup of books yet. I have a lot of surprises planned for 2021.

Thank you for reading my *47th* novel. (Wow, getting close to 50!) If you'd like to read more from me, check out my Amazon's author page. I write extreme horror and dark thriller novels. I suppose that's the best way to describe my work: *DARK*. If you think I won't go 'there,' think again. My next book is titled: *Am I Beautiful?* It's about a man who has a one-night stand with a young woman during a business trip to Tokyo, Japan. But the woman grows attached to him and threatens to tell his family about their affair. Drunk and desperate, the man beats her and mutilates her face before fleeing the country. Years later, he realizes his past has come back to haunt him... This book will work as a non-supernatural origin story for *Kuchisake-onna*—also known as The Slit-Mouthed Woman. It is one of my most creative, disturbing projects yet. I hope you'll go out and pre-order that, especially if you enjoyed my other horror 'romance' novels, such as *Lovesick* and *Maneater*. Once again, thank you for your support. I couldn't do this without you.

Until our next venture into the dark and disturbing,
Jon Athan

P.S. If you have any questions or comments, or if you're an aspiring author who needs *some* help, feel free to contact me directly using my business email: info@jon-athan.com. You can also contact me through Twitter @Jonny_Athan or my Facebook page. It might take me a while to get back to you, but I always try my best to respond. Thanks!

Printed in Great Britain
by Amazon